SPOOKED

MICHAEL E. BERG

120
pages

Printed in the United States of America

First Printing, 2017

ISBN-10: 1-947197-04-5
ISBN-13: 978-1-947197-04-6

120pages
Subway Sites LLC
PO BOX 231548
New York, NY 10023

120pages.com

HOW TO READ A SCREENPLAY

A screenplay is written to show, not tell. Screenplays convey how a film will play out. The story unfolds through the dialogue and actions of the characters. As such, words are used economically. There is less description than you would find in a novel, as those details are typically handled during the production process. There is very little exposition; the screenplay doesn't provide any information that an audience watching the film wouldn't receive.

Therefore, as you read, visualize a film in your mind and "see" it as if you were watching a film.

If you're not familiar with the screenplay format, here are some things to know:

SCENE HEADINGS

Scene headings describe where the action takes place, the time of day, and sometimes additional details, such as if the action takes place in a flashback or as part of a montage.

For example:

```
INT. SAMMY'S HOUSE - DAY
```

"INT" indicates the action is indoors. "SAMMY'S HOUSE" tells us the action is in a woman's house. "DAY" tells us that it is daytime.

```
EXT. PARK - NIGHT
```

"EXT" indicates the action is outdoors. "PARK" tells us we are in a park. "NIGHT" tells us that it is the evening.

Other time descriptions may be used, such as "SAME" to indicate action taking place simultaneously or "LATER" to indicate action taking place moments later, after a brief jump in time.

CAPITALIZED WORDS

Throughout a screenplay, you may come across CAPITALIZED WORDS. These generally indicate the introduction of a new character, that the camera should pay attention to a particular item/sound/person/location, or that we are moving into a specific place within the location.

For example:

```
John turns.  He sees SALLY, the most beautiful girl he has ever
laid eyes on.  In her hands, she holds AN ADORABLE PUPPY.
```

DIALOGUE

Dialogue is written by centering a character's name with their spoken words appearing beneath their name. For example:

```
                    JOHN
          You found Charlie!
```

PARANTHETICALS

Between the character's name and dialogue, you may see text in parenthesis. This indicates some specific direction about how the dialogue is to be read or some specific action that takes place during the delivery of the dialogue.

```
                    JOHN
               (eyes watering)
          You found Charlie!
```

OTHER TERMS

Here are some other terms you may come across when reading a screenplay:

(O.S.) or (O.C.) – Off-screen or off-camera indicates that we do not see a character when dialogue is heard

(V.O.) – Indicates voiceover. This is dialogue we hear, but the speaker is not physically present in the same location as the action

(CONT'D) – Indicates that the same character is continuing to deliver a line of dialogue after an action, scene change, or page break

(MORE) – Indicates that the dialogue from the character continues on the next page

POV – Indicates that we see the action through a defined point of view

SUPERIMPOSE – Indicates that we see text on screen, often to define a time or location

MONTAGE – Indicates rapid cutting of different scenes in a sequence, such as any training sequence in a Rocky movie

(beat) – Indicates that a character takes a brief pause before continuing dialogue

For Hannah, Ian, & Aidan

No matter how daunting it may seem,

never give up on your dreams.

FADE IN:

EXT. HOLLOW GROVE - NIGHT

Gliding through the sky over a tree-lined suburban
neighborhood below.

                    RADIO DJ (V.O.)
          That was "The Boys of Summer" by
          Don Henley, here on KZZQ 92.
          Spinning you the hits in another
          nonstop music hour.

A 1978 Oldsmobile Cutlass cruises into view.

SUPERIMPOSE: "Hollow Grove, PA - June 8, 1984"

INT. CUTLASS

The DRIVER resembles a love child of Wham and Huey Lewis. A
RADIO DJ voice crackles through the perforated speaker holes.

                    RADIO DJ (V.O.)
          It's nine-thirty and a balmy eighty-
          four degrees, but I'm not sweating
          it. Filled my pants with a dozen
          ice cubes.

                    DRIVER
          Less talk, more rock.

                    RADIO DJ (V.O.)
          A drier alternative would be our
          local bijou. Bill Murray's out with
          a new movie: Ghost Busters. A chill-
          thrill flick guaranteed to scare
          your socks off.

                    DRIVER
          Blah, blah, blah.

                    RADIO DJ (V.O.)
          For the rest of us, the heat keeps
          coming... in fact, it's on.

EERIE BELLS introduce...

                    DRIVER
          Yes! Love this song.

...a VACUOUS VOICE.

                    VACUOUS VOICE (O.S.)
          Me too.

2.

The Driver glances in his rearview mirror --

EXT. VICTORIAN MANOR

WAILING radiates from the Cutlass as it careens past THREE
TEENAGERS creaking up warped porch steps of the run-down
mansion.

FRANK PERIL, 13, leads the way in a Star Wars tank top
revealing muscle definition rarely seen for his age.

                    FRANK
          I just hope one us gets slimed
          tonight. Nothing would be cooler.

CHRIS GULLIFORD, 13, scrawnier with a cherub face and greased
back hair, tags close behind.

                    CHRIS
          You and me, Frank -- we're seeing
          it again! I'm not positive, but I
          think that Dana chick's boob popped
          out when monster hands felt her up.

                    FRANK
          Holding her down.

                    CHRIS
          Either way, boobage.

                    LIAM
          You two are mental. The movie blew.

LIAM SWINDAL, 15, wannabe roadie with a faux hawk and spiked
wristbands, unzips his backpack. Pulls out a crowbar and
flashlights.

                    LIAM
          Catching ghosts in a little box is
          bloody rubbish.

                    CHRIS
          Bloody rubbish, bloody rubbish --
          please stop already. You live in
          America.

                    LIAM
          For now. Until I become a rock god
          like David Bowie.

                    CHRIS
          Bowie's such a freak.

Liam lunges for Chris.

> LIAM
> Shut your cakehole, prat!

Frank blocks the attack.

> FRANK
> Take it easy, fish-n-chips. Stay
> focused on the plan.

> CHRIS
> Do we really need to go in?

Frank juts the crowbar under two rotted boards covering a
window...

> FRANK
> You agreed, Chris. Movie first,
> murder house after.

...and pries them off.

Liam shines the flashlight under his chin.

> LIAM
> Mur-der houuuuse. Oooo.

> CHRIS
> Please stop.

He redirects the light on Chris rubbing his ROSARY.

> LIAM
> Don't be a wuss.

INT. VICTORIAN MANOR - SITTING ROOM

The boys step into a sea of white sheets and cobwebs.

Flashlight beams reveal a lavish interior from another age.

> LIAM
> Posh.

Frank yanks a dust cover off a large painted FAMILY PORTRAIT
propped against the wall.

> FRANK
> I give you the Farringtons.

They study the unsettling realism.

> CHRIS
> *(shudders)*
> Gives me the creeps.

                         LIAM
              Which one went psycho?

                         FRANK
              The oldest son.

He pulls Chris to a rolltop desk. Hands him the flashlight.

Frank grips the handles and exerts a convincing display of
fruitless effort... runs his finger over the keyhole.

                         FRANK
              Liam.

Liam fishes from his pocket a crooked paper clip and
miniature screwdriver.

He manipulates the tools with methodical precision.

                         CHRIS
                    (sarcastic)
              Your Dad must be so proud.

CLICK.

                         LIAM
              He is.

Frank repositions himself.

                         FRANK
              Bet there's something important in
              here.

He slides the shutter up -- dozens of SPIDERS scatter
everywhere.

The boys jerk back, screaming, stamping... until squashed
spider guts litter the floor.

                         CHRIS
              That was gross.

                         FRANK
                    (breathes heavily)
              I'm gonna puke.

                         LIAM
              You look a bit peaked. Creepy
              crawlies give you the willies?

                         FRANK
              I hate spiders.

He spots a glint in the spider nest.

Summoning his courage, Frank reaches through the web and
retrieves a SKELETON KEY.

A windy HOWL whistles throughout the second floor.

                    CHRIS
          I want to go!

                    FRANK
          We woke the dead.

INT. VICTORIAN MANOR - DINING ROOM

Frank pushes the high double doors open.

He surveys with a macabre sense of awe. Drags the table cover
off.

                    FRANK
          Our best chance for contact.

They huddle around the table as Frank sets down a OUIJA
BOARD: pentagrams and ominous letters adorn the surface.

                    FRANK
          I picked this up from a shop in
          Salem last year.

                    LIAM
          Of course you did.

                    FRANK
          Each board is handmade with black
          magic.

                    CHRIS
          Black magic?

                    LIAM
          That doesn't even make sense.

Chris looks more worried and kisses his rosary.

                    LIAM
          Grow a set, why don't ya.

                    CHRIS
          It protects me from demons. Father
          Curry says the devil deals in black
          magic.

Liam laughs.

6.

                         LIAM
               You're so gullible, doofus.

                         CHRIS
               Prick.

                         LIAM
               Doofus.

                         CHRIS
               Prick!

Frank smacks the skeleton key down.

                         FRANK
               Shut - up. We don't have all night.

He places his fingers on the planchette.

                         FRANK
                    (commanding tone)
               I call upon any spirit in this
               house to join our table.

Silence.

                         FRANK
               Can we speak with Dr. Farrington?

Eerie stillness throughout the manor. Liam stretches.

                         LIAM
               Maybe the board's broken?

Chris seems perplexed, peeks under the table.

A long-haired, mangy KITTEN leaps up. Chris yelps and scoots
his chair back.

                         LIAM
               Where the hell did that come from?

The feline meows. Frank coaxes it over.

                         CHRIS
               Don't touch it. Probably has rabies
               or bad luck.

                         FRANK
               He's okay. Just creepin' for some
               attention. Aren't ya... Creepers.

Creepers purrs as Frank pets him.

                    LIAM
          Never give a bloody stray a name.

                    CHRIS
          Look!

The planchette rests on "hello."

                    LIAM
          Bollocks.

Frank anxiously touches the planchette again.

                    FRANK
          Dr. Farrington? Has someone made
          contact?

His hands jerk about the board spelling --

                    LIAM
          Ted? Bloody weak mate.

SLAP! Liam covers his cheek.

                    LIAM
          Ow!

                    FRANK
          Wicked cool.

                    CHRIS
          Holy-Mary-mother-of-Jesus.

Chris performs a Sign of the Cross and kisses his rosary.

                    FRANK
          Ted, did you hit Liam?

The planchette flies out from Frank's fingers to "YES."

                    FRANK
          This is getting good!

                    CHRIS
          I wanna leave, Frank. Please.

                    FRANK
          Not yet. Ted? Hello?

The key launches off the table!

Their breath turns to VAPOR.

Creepers arches his back and hisses.

The planchette whips about ON THE BOARD:

                    FRANK (O.S.)
          You... will... die.

A guttural, DEMONIC VOICE echoes the last word.

                    DEMONIC VOICE
          Die.

The boys SCREAM!

They scramble towards the entrance with Creepers scampering
after them.

Pictures drop off walls. Sheets leap into the air.

At the FRONT DOOR, Chris jiggles the ancient knob.

                    CHRIS
          It's locked!

Frank doubles back.

                    LIAM
          Where you going?!

He scavenges the floor.

                    FRANK
          Got it.

He holds up the skeleton key. An unseen force throws him
against the wall -- five feet off the floor!

Frank grapples at the air around his neck.

                    FRANK
          Help!

Chris and Liam are frozen in fear. Creepers growls.

Frank's face sinks in: appearing to shrivel like a tomato.

The SHADOW MIST, a black vaporish mass, materializes before
him.

                    DEMONIC VOICE
                (vicious laugh)
          Die.

A wet stain spreads over Liam's crotch.

Chris lobs an antique OIL LAMP through the Shadow Mist,
dispelling it.

Frank slumps to the floor. Creepers rubs up against his leg
while Chris tugs on Frank's arm.

                    CHRIS
          Get up! Move it! -- Liam!

He looks behind but sees no one.

                    CHRIS
          Liam split!

Frank regards Chris with drunken bewilderment.

                    FRANK
          Did he take my board?

                    CHRIS
          Screw the friggin' board!

Chris shakes Frank lucid and pulls him to the FRONT DOOR.

Frank fumbles with the key. The Shadow Mist coalesces over
his shoulder.

                    CHRIS
          Fraaaaaank!

EXT. VICTORIAN MANOR - NIGHT

The boys burst from the house, hollering as they flee.
Creepers tucked like a football in Frank's arm.

Behind them, the decaying entry slams shut.

                                        TO BLACK.

EXT. LENNY'S BIG STICK - NIGHT

Random VOICES and TRAFFIC noise. A neon sign blinks on:
"Lenny's Big   k"

SUPERIMPOSE: "June 10, 1997"

VIKRAM, 23, a hip-hop acclimating Indian, stands in front of
the seedy, two-story bar holding an 8mm CAMCORDER.

He peers through the EYEPIECE at a grainy image of FRANK, 26,
all-American good looks contrasted by a meager paunch; and
CHRIS, 26, styled bed head with smudged rocker guyliner.

They each wear jackets emblazoned by the "SPOOKED" logo: the
name with a cartoon ghost face in the center.

> CHRIS
> Welcome back to another thrilling
> episode of Spooked. Tonight we
> visit the illustrious pool hall and
> tavern, Lenny's Big Stick.

INT. LENNY'S BIG STICK - UPPER DECK

Chris stands next to KARL, a beer-stained, middle-aged man.

> CHRIS
> Lenny's second floor has been the
> hot spot for unusual disturbances.
> With me is the bar's forward
> thinking owner. Tell us, Karl,
> what's got everyone spooked?

Karl channels his inner Tony Robbins:

> KARL
> Real bizarre stuff, Chris. We've
> heard footsteps, loud noises, pool
> balls rolling off the tables.

> CHRIS
> Stuff not done by the drunkards,
> I'm guessing.

> KARL
> Definitely not the drunkards. We
> think it's Lenny, this place was
> his life.

> CHRIS
> Maybe he's pissed his life turned
> into such a dump. What do you
> think, Frank?

Karl scowls at Chris. Camcorder POV swings over to Frank.

> FRANK
> We'll set up, kill the lights, and
> see if Lenny's still tending bar.

INT. LENNY'S BIG STICK - UPPER DECK

NIGHT VISION mode. Frank holds two dowsing rods.

> FRANK
> Is anyone with us tonight?

Silence. Chris snaps flash photos.

                    CHRIS
          Hey, Lenny, I hear you make a zingy
          Rum Dinger.

                    FRANK
          What's our current temp?

Chris reads an infrared thermometer.

                    CHRIS
          A balmy eighty-five degrees.

                    FRANK
          I had Karl shut off the air. Should
          eliminate unwanted vent noise and
          false positives.

                    CHRIS
          You hear that? Sounds like score
          beads clicking.

They skulk forward as Frank whispers into Camcorder POV.

                    FRANK
          In my hands are dowsing rods, an
          ancient pagan tool. The rods will
          cross, like so, when concentrated
          levels of supernatural ener--

Pool cues CLATTER in the distance.

Chris dispatches to the noise. Camcorder POV jostles behind.

                    CHRIS
          Wha!

He suddenly slips from view -- FWUMP! -- groans.

Camcorder POV finds Chris sprawled on several pool cues, then
shifts to dowsing rods crossing over him.

                    FRANK
          Look at this! I'm picking up a
          major energy fluctuation.

                    CHRIS
          Fabulous. Call an ambulance. I
          broke my butt.

                    FRANK
          Your coccyx?

                              CHRIS
                    Let's hope not.

                              FRANK
                         (sighs)
                    Start looking for signs of
                    metaphysical residue.

Frank disappears into the dark...

He returns illuminated by a mounted fluorescent BLACK LIGHT.

                              FRANK
                         (to Camcorder POV)
                    We call this our Phantom Beacon.
                    The black light's ultraviolet
                    electromagnetic radiation will
                    illuminate past our world's
                    ethereal buffer into the spectral
                    plane. In theory, it attracts
                    spirits like bugs to a bug zapper.

He positions the Phantom Beacon on a pool table.

                              FRANK
                    Find anything?

                              CHRIS
                    Tons.

                              FRANK
                         (helps Chris up)
                    I feel like there's a presence
                    here. Let's start some EVP.

Chris speaks into a handheld tape recorder.

                              CHRIS
                    Mark 1:20 A.M., EVP session at the
                    Big Stick.

He balances it near the Phantom Beacon.

They pace the room...

                              FRANK
                    My name is Frank. We'd very much
                    like to meet you, Lenny. Come into
                    the light.

Silence.

                    CHRIS
          Help us, help you. Move an object.
          Do just one thing -- something big
          though, none of this little crap.

Silence.

                    FRANK
          Tell us what you want. We are here
          to listen.

Chris speaks into Camcorder POV.

                    CHRIS
          EVP, or Electronic Voice Phenomena
          is how we capture voices from the
          beyond. If we don't hear anything
          now, the tape track can be
          amplified on playback.

INT. LENNY'S BIG STICK - UPPER DECK - LATER

Chris sleeps curled up on the pool table. Frank's lower half
sticks out from under.

SUPERIMPOSE: "3:30 AM"

                    CHRIS
               (mumbles)
          No, no, Sister Agnes, not the
          knuckles.

Camcorder POV surveys the room. Stops on a wall. A DARK
FIGURE appears to run away.

                    VIKRAM (O.S.)
          Frank! Frank!

                    CHRIS
          It wasn't me!

Frank crawls out, yawning.

                    VIKRAM (O.S.)
          Check over by the door. I saw
          movement.

                    FRANK
          Chris?

Chris points the infrared thermometer.

                    CHRIS
                 (excited)
        Seventy-five, four... seventy-one.
        Got a crazy cold spot anomaly:
        eight degrees cooler. Amazing.

EXT. LENNY'S BIG STICK

Camcorder POV zooms in on Frank's face, zoom's out, focuses.

                    FRANK
        We wrapped up the session. Had
        unusual and spooky activity
        tonight. My gut feeling is
        something with intelligence lingers
        here for some reason.

The image changes to Telemundo -- Home Shopping Network --
Jerry Springer.

INT. PUBLIC ACCESS TV - DAY

Jerry Springer plays on a wall-mounted TV in an empty
reception room.

SUPERIMPOSE: "October 6, 1997"

CAROLINA, 31, a feisty Latina with hoop earrings, laughs from
behind her desk as she files long false nails. Points her
emery board at the TV.

                    CAROLINA
        Oh no you didn't!

She pushes a blinking button and cradles the headset.

                    CAROLINA
        Channel 14, how can I help you?

Chris strolls up in his favorite Green Day "dookie" t-shirt:
right arm sleeved by a collage of punk rock tattoos.

He drum rolls the counter, flashing a bravado smile.

Carolina snaps her fingers and directs him down the hall.

                    CAROLINA
        You're late. Studio A. Vamanos!

                    CHRIS
        Gracias, bonita receptionista.

Chris hurries towards a glowing red light.

                    CAROLINA (O.S.)
          No, pendejo, Glenda doesn't make
          house calls!

Inside STUDIO A, an array of STAFF and SHOW PERSONALITIES
fill out rows of folding chairs. SHARON, 50, a plump station
manager with beehive hair, stands before them.

Chris lets go of the heavy stage door.

                    SHARON
          Here to explain more about --

THUD!

All eyes focus on him.

LIAM, 28, intercepts in a pinstripe suit with spiked orange
hair and a hoop earring.

                    LIAM
          Tosspots aren't wanted here.

Over his shoulder, Sharon asserts.

                    SHARON
          Grab a seat Chris, we just started.

                    CHRIS
               (scoffs)
          Nice hair.

He steps past Liam and makes a passing leer at GLENDA, 42 --
Jessica Rabbit incarnate -- and her buxom, button-straining
cleavage.

She catches his eye line and winks.

Chris trips over his feet, banging into a chair as he drops.
Pulls himself up next to Frank.

                    SHARON
          Please welcome our very special
          guest: Kitty Clausen.

Sharon claps with the audience as KITTY CLAUSEN, 38,
approaches the podium in her corporate attire.

                    KITTY
          Thank you, Sharon. Hello, everyone.
          For those who don't know me, I'm a
          producer for The Reality Channel.

This sparks murmuring among the attendees. Chris nudges Frank
and paws at the air like a cat.

                    KITTY
          With the recent acquisition of
          Channel 14, our CEO has tasked me
          to assess your station's lineup for
          the next several weeks. We're
          hoping one of you will be our next
          water cooler hit. The chosen show
          receives a cash incentive and
          national airtime on TRC.

INT. PUBLIC ACCESS TV - RECEPTION

Chris and Frank face off against Liam in a crowded lobby;
while Sharon escorts Kitty around for the meet and greet.

                    CHRIS
          Cheerio, carrot top.

                    LIAM
          Cheerio means goodbye, you prat.

                    FRANK
          What's the latest, Liam? I mean,
          besides getting jumped by a
          pumpkin.

                    LIAM
          It's Bowie's latest look.

                    FRANK
          Way to be your own person.

                    LIAM
          My protege approves.

                    CHRIS
          Satan?

Liam beckons to BROOKE HALLSTROM, 23, flowing hair and narrow-
rimmed glasses distract from her willful intelligence.

Time slows down as Frank gazes at Brooke crossing the room.

Liam rests his hands on her shoulders.

                    LIAM
          Brooke, love.

Brooke shrugs him off, but gives the other two a warm smile.

                    BROOKE
          I'm your new programmer, and a fan.

                    CHRIS
          What happened to Charlie?

                    LIAM
          The little bugger took a job with
          PBS: four months ago.

Frank becomes flustered with embarrassment from Liam's
divulgence.

                    FRANK
          Spooked has been on a, um,
          hiatus... lately.

                    LIAM
          Staring at the bloody walls all
          night.

                    CHRIS
          Bloody walls? We'd be so lucky.

                    BROOKE
          I have a few ideas for the show, if
          you trust it in my hands.

                    FRANK
          Definitely.

                    CHRIS
          Handle me anytime, Brooke. Even
          after we get on TRC.

                    BROOKE
          So the TV personality isn't an act.
          Good to know.

                    LIAM
          No network would ever hire a couple
          of nutters.

                    CHRIS
          That's harsh.

                    LIAM
          Casper doesn't exist, and you'll
          never prove otherwise.

                    CHRIS
          Gauntlet accepted.

                    FRANK
          Stay right there, Brooke. We'll be
          back with Spooked-tacular footage
          before you can say --

                    CHRIS
          Boo.

Brooke hides her amusement as she watches them leave.

EXT. PUBLIC ACCESS TV - PARKING

Chris beams with enthusiasm as he and Frank weave around cars
crammed together on the cracked lot.

                    CHRIS
          Alright! Time to mobilize. What's
          the game plan?

                    FRANK
          Go home, play Nintendo.

                    CHRIS
               (frustrated)
          But you just said --

                    FRANK
          I couldn't let orange crush have
          the last word.

                    CHRIS
          Well yeah, but now's our chance!

                    FRANK
          To do what? The well is dry. We've
          hit all our usual spots -- twice.

                    CHRIS
          There's gotta be other places,
          better places. Let's try thinking
          over the box.

CLINKITY-CLANK.

                    GLENDA (O.S.)
          Damnit.

The guys spot Glenda near her convertible. Chris goes slack-
jawed.

                    CHRIS
          Meeting adjourned.

Glenda provides an unwitting show from her rising skirt as
she strains to reach her keys.

                    GLENDA
          Hi, boys. Chris-ta-pher, will you
          come over here?

                    FRANK
          Should I wait?

                    CHRIS
          With a damsel in distress? Can't
          rush chivalry -- I've got my pass.

Chris pockets his bus pass as he swaggers over to Glenda.

She pouts at the ground.

                    GLENDA
          Do you mind?

                    CHRIS
          It'd be my pleasure.

He crouches down, admiring the barelegged view.

                    GLENDA
          Such the gentleman. You must not
          have banged it too hard.

He places the keys in her hand.

                    CHRIS
          Excuse me?

                    GLENDA
          When your knee hit the chair.

                    CHRIS
          Oh right. No, it's fine, I'm fine,
          you're... healthy.

Chris ogles, hypnotized.

                    GLENDA
                (adjusts her breasts)
          Honestly, Christopher, you've no
          idea what a burden my body can be.

                    CHRIS
          I'm a quick study.

She slinks in behind the steering wheel and fits on a pair of
oversized sunglasses.

                         GLENDA
               I'd give you a ride, but Roger
               should be home soon. He likes when
               I greet him in my special chef's
               apron: it's sheer.

INT. APT - FRANK'S BEDROOM - MORNING

Frank's steely eyes open to PURRING and LICKING. They shift
up at the now fluffier, well-fed Creepers resting on top of
his head.

His room reflects an obsession with "Ghostbusters" and
paranormal studies: Cast-signed poster. Parapsychology
Correspondence Course Diploma.

He relocates the cat to his Stay Puft comforter and frowns at
seeing "8:01" on the bedside Zuul Tower clock.

Creepers leans in for a welcomed ear scratch.

                         FRANK
               What good are you? I'm late for
               work.

Frank nuzzles his nose against the cat's.

                         FRANK
               Worthless kitty.

INT. GAS N GRUB - SAME

A long line of irritable CUSTOMERS stand at the register of a
middle-aged FRAZZLED HAIR CLERK. She glares over at --

Chris slouching behind a "Register Closed" sign. He holds a
partially eaten banana and sips from his 64 oz. "Bladder
Buster Super Gulp."

Frazzled Hair Clerk slams the cash register drawer. Chris
looks to her, then the clock. He removes the sign.

                         CHRIS
               I can help whoever.

A swarm of people shift over.

INT. APT - LATER

Wearing blue jeans and a loose shirt, Frank passes Creepers
sitting by an empty bowl. The cat meows.

Frank doubles back.

He dishes up a cup of dry cat food.

                    FRANK
          Guard the castle.

EXT. APT - PARKING

A "No Pets Allowed" entrance door swings open.

Pop-Tart in mouth, Frank bounds down the cement stairs to his
battered '89 Pontiac Sunbird.

EXT. SERVICE CENTER - DAY

The Sunbird rolls into a reserved parking stall at a mundane
beige building plastered with the words "Service Center."

INT. SERVICE CENTER

Cubicle hell as far as the eye can see.

Frank sips from a "Gas N Grub" coffee cup as he passes under
the Wizard of Oz themed banner: "Follow our Yellow Brick Road
to Success."

Blowhard laughter fills the air.

                    CYRUS (O.S.)
          Frank, get in here!

Frank moseys into CYRUS'S OFFICE, the sanctuary of an avid
Doberman Pinscher owner.

CYRUS, 40s, an imposing black man with a belt-busting belly,
leans back in his leather lumbar chair.

                    CYRUS
          Look what the cat dragged in.
               (shakes head)
          Must be trippin', clock says five
          after nine.

                    FRANK
          Overslept.

                    CYRUS
          Time you decide what's more
          important: a career or unemployment
          check.

Cyrus locks his hands in pompous impatience while Frank chugs
his remaining coffee.

                    FRANK
          That's a tough choice. I'll mull it
          over.

                    CYRUS
          Let's hope so. For now, get me a
          breakdown of your team's earnings
          from last month -- ready for
          today's eleven o'clock.

AT HIS DESK, Frank drops into the squeaky pseudo-ergonomic
chair. Relocates a stack of folders off his keyboard.

                    FRANK
          Morning, people.

A few TEAM MEMBERS wave from down the aisle of misfit
collectors. Vikram touches his headset and spins around.

                    VIKRAM
          Check it, Frank.
               (holds up CD case)
          Got Snoopy Dog Dog on heavy
          rotation.

                    FRANK
          Slammin'. Just keep the rap stuff
          to a minimum, when on the phone.

                    VIKRAM
          Fo shizzle.

He swivels back.

Frank sulks over his mountain of paperwork, makes a call.

                    FRANK
          Chris, it's me... *Frank*. How much
          flour do we have?

MONTAGE - "JUST MISSED" GHOST INVESTIGATIONS

INT. RETIREMENT HOME - HALLWAY - NIGHT

Frank and Chris cover the floor in flour.

An ELDERLY MAN hobbles out and slips. As they help him,
FOOTPRINTS walk past.

INT. DORMITORY ROOM - NIGHT

Chris and Frank lounge on a futon, bathed in their own black
light.

A pair of pretty COEDS wave as they pass by. Chris stalks after them. Frank reluctantly follows.

The wind chimes CLANG. A shimmery WOMAN silently floats in with her faced etched by a terror-stricken scream.

EXT. FARM - NIGHT

The guys roam past several haystacks. They mill among the cows and attempt to tip one over.

Behind them, a MANIACAL PITCHFORK tosses hay everywhere.

END MONTAGE

INT. APT - DAY

BEEPS and BOOPS play over an 8-bit synthesized music track. A grease-stained pizza box lays open on the kitchen bar.

      FRANK (O.S.)
  Hey, Brooke. Like the new footage?
  Oh...

The taut phone cord stretches across to Frank perched on the sofa arm, phone cradled to his ear.

      FRANK
  Hmm, okay. Bye.

His shoulder drops and the phone springs back. Frank slides onto the cushion, rapidly tapping his game controller.

      FRANK
  Brooke says our new stuff is
  lacking.

Clunky "Ghostbusters NES" graphics side-scroll across the TV.

Chris juggles a slice of pizza as he plays.

      CHRIS
    (offended)
  In what?

      FRANK
  The thing that makes people talk at
  water coolers apparently.

      CHRIS
  Maybe it's time we go back to the
  house.

Frank glances at Chris who's become considerably pale.

> FRANK
> Your bravery's admirable but the
> property was condemned last year.
> City probably tore it down.

EXT. VICTORIAN MANOR - NIGHT

A pristine '96 Ford Mustang stops in front of the fully
landscaped and renovated mansion.

INT. VICTORIAN MANOR

Brooke sets her bags down in a lavish foyer. MORMA, 76, an
artifact from the old country, gives her a hug.

> MORMA
> Welcome home, child.

> BROOKE
> Something smells yummy. I'm
> starved.

INT. VICTORIAN MANOR - DINING ROOM

Morma, Brooke, and BOBBY, 16, moody; sit around a carved
walnut table topped with home cooked goodness.

NADINE, 47, proper wife and timeless beauty, sets the final
dish.

> NADINE
> There. Is everyone washed, ready to
> eat?

> BROOKE
> Mmm-hmm.

Nadine directs her attention to Bobby.

> BOBBY
> Why you always looking at me?

> NADINE
> Because I know Brooke is very
> thorough in her hygiene.

> BOBBY
> Thorough? She's a freak about it!

> NADINE
> That's enough. Off you go. Your
> father --

JOHAN HALLSTROM, 56, a silver-haired executive, strides past
Bobby.

                    JOHAN
          Hello, family. Where's Bobby
          headed?

                    NADINE
          Bathroom.

                    BROOKE
          Make sure you wash for thirty
          seconds. I'm timing you.

                    NADINE
          Brooke.

                    BROOKE
          What? You know how he is. It's
          disgusting.

                    JOHAN
          Brooke, honey, all teenage boys are
          disgusting.

He kisses the top of Morma's head.

          JOHAN   SUBTITLE
Nattvarden ser underbart,   Supper looks wonderful,
Mamma.   Mamma.

Nadine leans back for one on the lips.

Johan settles in at the table as Bobby returns. The meal
commences.

                    JOHAN
          Any new developments transpire at
          the station?

                    BROOKE
          I've been assisting Kitty on
          several tasks.

                    JOHAN
          Excellent. You can learn a lot from
          her.

                    BROOKE
          And had the opportunity to work on
          new material from Spooked.

26.

MORMA
(broken English)
What is Spooked?

BROOKE
It's a show, Grandma, about
investigating ghosts.

Johan rolls his eyes as he eats.

NADINE
Have you met them in person?

BOBBY
No one cares.

BROOKE
A few times. Chris can be so
conceited. But Frank, Frank's...
sweet.

NADINE
We're *all* very happy for you,
honey.

Johan fakes an enthusiastic grunt.

INT. VICTORIAN MANOR - BEDROOM - LATER

Brooke wanders into a room with pastel colors and generic
framed art.

She flips on the light to a closet filled with clothes and
stacked boxes. Starts sifting through the boxes on a shelf.

BROOKE
Mom? Which box has grandma's
photos?

A dusty GAME BOARD bonks her on the head.

BROOKE
Ow! What the hell.

She picks up the board and planchette piece. Wipes off a
layer of dust: it's Frank's Ouija board from 1984.

Her fingers become caked in grime.

BROOKE
Eww, gross.

Brooke pulls a mini Purell bottle from her pocket. Gooey
sanitizer oozes out. She rubs frantically to no avail.

                    BROOKE
          Bobby! Bobby!

                    BOBBY (O.S.)
          What?

                    BROOKE
          Come up here, please. Bring me a
          wet cloth.

                    BOBBY (O.S.)
          Get it yourself!

                    NADINE (O.S.)
          Bobby Johan! Do as your sister has
          asked.

Bobby CLOMPS his way up.

                    BOBBY
          Here.

He tosses the washcloth and turns.

                    BROOKE
          Not so fast.

Bobby mopes forward.

                    BOBBY
                (whiny)
          What...

Brooke cleans her hands more than the board.

                    BROOKE
          Did you stash this in my room?

                    BOBBY
          Guest bedroom.

                    BROOKE
          Don't get smart, doesn't suit you.
          I used to play Ouija in college. It
          makes contact with spirits.

                    BOBBY
          Sounds lame.

                    BROOKE
          Let's try it.

                    BOBBY
          Let's not.

                    BROOKE
          You think Mom knows about a certain
          Swedish Bikini Team pictorial in
          the bathroom?

                    BOBBY
          Huh? You didn't -- it's not mine.

He closes the door.

                    BROOKE
          You know those girls aren't really
          from Sweden.

                    BOBBY
          Don't care.

Brooke lights a scented candle. Flips the bedroom light off.

She sets out the Ouija board on her bed.

                    BROOKE
          Place your fingers like so -- don't
          touch mine!

Bobby mocks her but does as commanded.

                    BROOKE
          Is there a presence with us?

The planchette slides over to "Yes."

Brooke shudders. She checks behind her.

                    BROOKE
          I have goosebumps! What's your
          name?

                    OUIJA BOARD
               (spells)
          T-E-D.

Bobby laughs.

                    BOBBY
          Hello, Ted! Really, Brooke, how
          dumb do you think I am?

                    BROOKE
          You try. Ask anything.

                    BOBBY
          Will my sister ever move out?

                    BROOKE
          How sweet.

The board piece moves to "No."

                    BOBBY
          Are you kidding? Gonna stay a
          freeloading moocher?

                    BROOKE
          I'll get my own place, one day.
          Takes a bit longer to achieve than
          a high score.

                    BOBBY
          Whatever. Okie-dokie "Ted," why
          not?

                    OUIJA BOARD
               (spells)
          D-E-A-D.

Brooke's horrified.

                    BROOKE
          Bobby!

                    BOBBY
          What? Blame Ted. Ted says you're
          dead. Ted says you're dead.

The door swings open. Candle blows out. Brooke shrieks!

A hallway SHADOW spills into the room.

                    BROOKE
          Grandma, you scared me half-to-
          death.

Morma frowns at the board.

                    MORMA
          Time for bed. School tomorrow.

Bobby stretches, yawns. He kisses Morma's cheek and makes his
escape.

Morma leaves. Her shadow follows seconds later.

INT. SERVICE CENTER - CUBICLE ROW - DAY

Green characters fill up predefined spaces on a monochromatic
screen until --

TAP, TAP... TAP, TAP... TAP, TAP, TAP!

The cursor blinks, refusing to move.

Vikram lets loose a flurry of Hindi curses.

Frank looks up from him magazine, "Mysteries of the Realm," rubbing his temples.

                    FRANK
          Whoa, Vik, take it down a notch.

QUINN, 30, bald and burly, fills the aisle with his imposing frame.

                    QUINN
          The whole building can hear you.

                    VIKRAM
          My keyboard's dead, dog.

He pounds the keys.

UNDER THE DESK, Quinn shimmies himself behind the PC and finds a loose keyboard cable. He pulls the power cord.

                    VIKRAM
          Now it's gone!

                    QUINN
          Looks serious. This might take
          awhile.

Frank shuffles through a mess of paper.

                    FRANK
          Jerry's out today. You can use his
          machine.

Vikram gathers up his portable CD player.

                    VIKRAM
          Fo rizzle? Jerry's desk stinks of
          old yogurt cups and chew spit. Make
          it fast, Quinn!

He kicks Quinn's boot sole, but gets no response.

Quinn stays focused on FRANK'S MONITOR where a web page scrolls down to "Pennsylvania Ghost Stories: Last Curtain Call at Hollow Grove's Middle School."

                    QUINN
          Whatchya working on?

The monitor blinks off. Frank tosses Quinn the magazine.

                    FRANK
          Stupid stuff. Just killing time.

INT. VICTORIAN MANOR - LIVING ROOM - DAY

Bobby deposits his book bag.

                    BOBBY
               (hollers)
          Mom, I'm home. Gonna improve my
          hand-eye coordination for awhile.

He nestles into a leather rocker game chair, holding an
orange light gun.

"House of the Dead" buzzes on a mammoth 60" TV. The game
starts.

Bobby shoots wildly at the screen.

                    BOBBY
          Take that. Ha, you missed. Brain
          splatter! Not on my watch.

Greyish-black WISPS OF SMOKE pour from the fireplace and
glide through the room.

They converge behind Bobby into a vaporish mass. The Shadow
Mist reaches out when --

Bobby leaps from his chair.

                    BOBBY
          No! C'mon! I shot him.

He cocks his head, looks behind: nothing's there.

                    BOBBY
          Huh.

THE VIDEO GAME resumes play. Roving crosshairs blow zombies
to bits. The remaining zombies slow in unison, all facing
directly at the screen.

BOBBY pulls the trigger but gets blanks. He lowers his gun
and inches forward.

                    BOBBY
          What the?

A mass of ZOMBIES group together.

They press closer and closer until their pixilated faces fill the screen.

                    ZOMBIES
          We see you, Bobby.

                    BOBBY
                 (frightened)
          Mom! Mom! Mom!

He bolts from the room.

EXT. VICTORIAN MANOR

Nadine clips dead branches off a rose bush in her designer gardening attire.

Bobby leans over the banister.

                    BOBBY
          Mommmmm! My game's possessed!

Nadine points her shears at Bobby.

                    NADINE
          This proves you spend too much time
          in front of the TV. Come outside
          and oxygenate your brain with fresh
          air.

                    BOBBY
          No, Mom. I'm serious.

                    NADINE
          I could use help pruning my plants.

                    BOBBY
          The zombies said my name. They're
          not even suppose to talk!

Nadine brushes off her garden apron.

                    NADINE
          I'm coming in, but for my ice tea.

INT. VICTORIAN MANOR - LIVING ROOM

Ominous music blares from the TV's static game menu.

Nadine marches in, scans the room.

                    NADINE
          Well?

Bobby peeks around the corner.

                    NADINE
          For heaven's sake, Bobby, get in
          here.

He moseys to the TV, flabbergasted.

                    BOBBY
          Wait, this wasn't -- the zombies
          looked right at me and said
          "Bobby."

                    NADINE
          That's quite enough young man. You
          are banned from playing this stupid
          game for two weeks.

Nadine puzzles over the rat nest of cords connected to a
power strip.

                    BOBBY
          What? You can't. C'mon, Mom.

Frustrated, she yanks the Saturn off its power cord.

                    NADINE
          Two weeks.

She carries the game system away.

EXT. MIDDLE SCHOOL - NIGHT

A persistent downpour.

SUPERIMPOSE: "October 15 - 10:00 PM"

Two figures emerge from the Sunbird. They splash across the
courtyard to a lighted entrance.

INT. MIDDLE SCHOOL

LEXI ERWIN, 20s, former cheer captain brimming with perky
enthusiasm, greets them.

                    LEXI
          Hi there. Such lovely weather we're
          having.

Frank and Chris shake themselves like wet dogs. Then peel off
their jackets.

                    LEXI
          Let me take your coats.

She hangs them on a nearby coat rack.

                    CHRIS
               (whispers)
          Yummy.

                    LEXI
          My name's Lexi. Who is who?

                    FRANK
          I'm Frank. He's Chris. Thanks for
          meeting us tonight.

                    LEXI
          Brooke sparked my interest. She
          said you catch ghosts?

Frank rummages through his bag. Pulls out the infrared
thermometer.

                    FRANK
          Investigate hauntings. Documenting
          the existence of supernatural
          entities.

                    CHRIS
               (charming cockiness)
          For our show on channel 14.

                    LEXI
          Niiice.

As they walk down a HALLWAY, Lexi notices many of Chris's
tattoos.

                    LEXI
          Your arm is so colorful.

                    FRANK
          Like a peacock.

Chris scowls at Frank...

                    LEXI
          Or an unfinished work of art.

...and beams at Lexi.

                    CHRIS
          I'm always finding an excuse to add
          another.

                    LEXI
          I have just the one. It's kind of
          silly.

She twists her wrist over to reveal "Smurfette playing a
flute."

                    CHRIS
          That's bad ass. She looks hot -- to
          other Smurfs.

Lexi blushes.

Frank senses his third-wheel status.

                    FRANK
          Brooke never mentioned what you
          teach.

                    LEXI
          Music.

                    CHRIS
          I love music!

She pushes open the AUDITORIUM double doors and proceeds down
an aisle.

                    LEXI
          Chorus, specifically. But I plan on
          starting a swing choir unit in the
          spring.

They climb up the stage steps.

                    CHRIS
          This brings back memories.

                    FRANK
          I'm not reading any temperature
          shift. Where was the phantom seen?

He unpacks the remaining equipment.

                    LEXI
          I can't be sure it was an actual
          ghost, but during our school assem--

                    CHRIS
          Wait! Frank, shouldn't we get this
          for the opening?
               (to Lexi)
          Do you mind? Being filmed?

                    LEXI
          Not at all.

                    CHRIS
          Great. Just stand by me, and I'll
          do the rest.

CAMCORDER POV centers Chris and Lexi in the frame. Lexi
claps.

                    LEXI
          So exciting.

The red light blinks on.

                    CHRIS
          Welcome back to another episode of
          Spooked. Tonight we focus on a
          middle school mystery -- no, not
          the lunches. With us is Lexi Erwin,
          the school's talented music
          teacher.

INT. SERVICE CENTER - DAY

A sleep-deprived Frank checks his PAGER as he punches in a
number on a fax machine. Vikram interrupts him.

                    VIKRAM
          Keeping it real, Frank?

                    FRANK
          Like every other day.

                    VIKRAM
          Fo shizzle.

The machine chirps on and feeds a crudely drawn CEMETERY
MAP...

INT. MUSTANG - NIGHT

...that rests on Brooke's leather passenger seat.

EXT. CEMETERY

Headlight beams lead the Mustang through an open gate and
over a hill.

The Mustang parks next to an overgrown willow tree. Thick fog
envelops Brooke as she crosses to the Sunbird.

                    BROOKE
          Frank?

On the hood is a flashlight with a note: "Use me."

She clicks it on and creeps among the graves.

EXT. CEMETERY - CRYPT

Brooke highlights a big crayon "X" on the side of a weathered tomb.

> BROOKE
> Cute, Frank. X marks the spot. But
> where's my treasure?

> FRANK
> *(lights up face)*
> Right here.

Brooke squeals.

> BROOKE
> Was that really necessary?

> FRANK
> Goes with the territory. I am a
> ghost hunter.

> BROOKE
> Could of done without the fog.

> FRANK
> Helps set the mood.

He circles the crypt, lighting a candle perched on each corner.

Brooke can't help but feel flattered.

> BROOKE
> In what way, exactly?

> FRANK
> Uh... here's the tape.

He puts a VIDEO8 TAPE on the stone slab.

> BROOKE
> Will I be impressed?

His enthusiasm goes on auto-pilot.

                         FRANK
               It's our biggest find yet!
               I'm ninety-nine percent sure we
               captured a metaphysical
               manifestation on film.

                         BROOKE
               No way! I can't wait to see this.

                         FRANK
               No waiting required.

Frank illuminates a POLAROID PHOTO.

                         FRANK
               It's a little fuzzy, but if you
               look by the curtain...

                         BROOKE
               Awe-some!

She wraps him in a big hug and lets go just as fast.

                         BROOKE
               But why meet in a graveyard?

Frank rests against the crypt.

                         FRANK
               This place holds special
               significance.

                         BROOKE
               Dead relative?

                         FRANK
               My first investigation.

                         BROOKE
               Wasn't that in the old lady's
               kitchen?

                         FRANK
               Way before Mrs. Vine and her
               reincarnated-dead-husband-pet-rat
               Mortimer.

                         BROOKE
               Forgot he had a name.

                         FRANK
               Back in high school, I wanted to
               capture footage of Mr. Stantz. He's
               the cemetery's oldest resident.

Brooke examines the stone but sees no discernible markings.

> BROOKE
> Are you sure it's him? The etchings
> have completely worn.

> FRANK
> Legend says Stantz died here after -
> -

> BROOKE
> Lightning struck him down!

> FRANK
> Nothing that dramatic.

> BROOKE
> Oh.

FLASHBACK - DEATH OF MR. STANTZ

[Shown as scratchy, deteriorated black & white film]

EXT. OPEN FIELD - DAY (1893)

MR. STANTZ leads a group of DISTINGUISHED GENTLEMEN in top
hats with his walking stick.

> FRANK (V.O.)
> While Stantz surveyed the land with
> investors, he took a bad step...

Mr. Stantz tumbles out of sight.

The Gentlemen peer down a DEEP HOLE and see Mr. Stantz laying
face down, looking up.

> FRANK (V.O.)
> ...and broke his neck.

> BROOKE (V.O.)
> That sucks.

EXT. CEMETERY - CRYPT - NIGHT (1997)

> FRANK
> For all we know, they just left him
> there.

> BROOKE
> Why not? He's already dead. Throw a
> little dirt on him and call it
> good.

They share a laugh.

> FRANK
> People claim a ghostly man wanders
> the cemetery in a top hat, but I've
> never seen him. Thought maybe
> tonight...

Brooke gazes receptively at Frank.

He loses himself in her eyes.

She leans forward...

Frank opens his mouth -- erupts into a COUGHING FIT.

He recovers and discerns a lipstick-sized tube of Binaca in Brooke's hand.

> BROOKE
> Sorry. Fresh breath and all.

She spritzes her own mouth.

More hesitant now, Frank eases in until their lips touch for a lingering, tender kiss.

Brooke suddenly recoils. He flushes, dumbfounded.

> BROOKE
> No tongue on the first date.

INT. SERVICE CENTER - FRANK'S ROW - DAY

HAROLD, 68, a former retiree who favors tweed jackets, sets down his headset and rubs his eyes underneath a pair of bifocals.

Frank slouches in the CONFERENCE ROOM among other TEAM LEADS. He doodles ghosts in a notepad while Cyrus scribbles on the whiteboard.

Harold's steps echo in an empty BATHROOM as he passes several sinks and stalls until opening the last door.

IN THE STALL, Harold flips open a newspaper. Sounds of running water and WHISTLING surprise him.

He listens... a second faucet starts. A third.

> HAROLD
> Hello? Who's out there?

WATER gushes from all three sinks in unison...

                         HAROLD (V.O.)
                Turn off the tap.

HAROLD reads over the funnies section.

A toilet flushes. Then another. He peers underneath the panel
but sees nothing.

                         HAROLD
                What the devil?
                     (calls out)
                Joke's over. I'll make sure
                management hears --

From the HALLWAY, we hear a distraught YELL. Harold waddles
out, pants around his legs.

INT. VICTORIAN MANOR - KITCHEN - DAY

Immaculate granite and stainless steel everything. Nadine
stands at the island among various ingredients surrounding a
KitchenAid mixer.

A cookbook lays propped open to "Double Layer Pumpkin
Cheesecake."

Nadine picks up a bottle of vanilla extract, shrugs, and
pours an unmeasured amount in. She sets the large beater on a
slow figure eight pattern. Leafs through her Cosmopolitan.

The Shadow Mist filters out from a floor vent.

It collects underneath Nadine's dress. A MIST HAND caresses
her leg.

She sets the magazine down, examines her calf.

                         NADINE
                Hmm, missed a spot.

The Shadow Mist seeps into an electrical outlet shared with
the mixer.

The KitchenAid ramps up in speed. Nadine glances over,
joggles the control switch. She panics. Turns it off.

The beater whips about at a blinding pace! Batter ejects from
the bowl in all directions.

Nadine pulls the cord but nothing happens. She shrieks!

Morma appears.

                         MORMA
                     (broken English)
              What is the matter, dear?

The KitchenAid has stopped.

Nadine stares wide-eyed, splattered in batter. She wipes a
chunk off her face, tastes it, unable to express what she's
feeling.

                         NADINE
              Needs more cinnamon.

INT. SERVICE CENTER - CYRUS'S OFFICE

Frank and Harold are seated before a confounded Cyrus.

                         CYRUS
              Let me get this straight. A ghost
              scared you off the toilet?

                         HAROLD
              Correct. And he whistled.

                         CYRUS
              Whistling ghost... Harold, are you
              high? Doped up on Percoset,
              Oxycotin, Augmentin, Viagra?

                         HAROLD
              No, sir. I do take aspirin from
              time to time when my hip flares up.

                         CYRUS
              Go home, Harold, get some rest. You
              can make up the hours tomorrow.

Harold shakes his head as he leaves. Frank stands...

                         CYRUS
              We're not done.

...and sits back down.

                         CYRUS
              Pranking your own team member is
              unprofessional, especially the old
              fart.

                         FRANK
              Wasn't me. Office antics are always
              done to one's superior.

                    CYRUS
          I won't let you make a mockery of
          this office.

                    FRANK
          Outside of the norm.

                    CYRUS
          Listen up. If I ever learn you and
          that loudmouth degenerate were
          snooping around here: you're gone.

INT. PUBLIC ACCESS TV - EDITING ROOM

Liam's reclined, feet up, earmuff headphones on. Transfixed
by a video of Glenda picking tomatoes in her barely-there
bikini top as she spills out of low-slung garden bibs.

Kitty sneaks up behind Liam and taps his shoulder.

He jerks, removing the headphones.

                    LIAM
          Bloody hell, Kitty. You startled
          me.

                    KITTY
          What exactly are you watching?

                    LIAM
          Editing, Glenda's latest tape.

                    KITTY
          Why is she dressed so...

                    LIAM
          Freely? Consider her former life as
          a burlesque dancer -- old habits
          and all.

Kitty pulls out the headphones' jack. Glenda's voice fills
the room.

                    GLENDA (O.S.)
          Before plucking it off the vine, we
          should check for ripeness.

On the VIDEO, Glenda fondles a juicy, red tomato. She shifts
her position and obscures the plant with her own luscious
melons.

                    GLENDA
          Hold them in your hand. Feel the
          weight. Are they heavy?

Her bosom heaves. Muffled snickers.

> GLENDA
> Gently squeeze. You want them to
> feel soft and plump.

Kitty switches the monitor off.

> KITTY
> I can't believe Sharon allows such
> crass programming.

Liam chuckles, leans back.

> LIAM
> She's our most requested show. And
> Glenda does know her veggies. I've
> sampled many: quite tasty.

> KITTY
> It's public access porn.

> LIAM
> Glenda holds the greatest chance
> for a national audience. She'll
> have a lock on the eighteen to
> forty-year-old demographic. Imagine
> how much ad revenue that will
> generate.

Kitty mulls over his pitch.

> KITTY
> Are you sleeping with her?

> LIAM
> No, but I've lined up a dozen
> companies ready to back her launch.
> TRC needs me.

INT. GAS N GRUB - NIGHT

Chris plays solitaire on the counter.

JENNY BITTERMAN, 20s, glam rock girl with pink hair and a
nose ring, checks off inventory on a clipboard.

BUH-BING.

Frank beelines for the Hostess aisle...

> FRANK
> Grab your stuff!

...finds "Twinkies" and "Sno Balls."

Jenny glances over, not losing count.

                    JENNY
          What's going on, Frank?

He scavenges the shelf.

                    FRANK
          New possibilities... damn it.

Frank pops his head over the row. He displays a crumpled,
crusty, CUPCAKE package.

                    FRANK
               (to Chris)
          Is this all you've got?

                    JENNY
          Our next shipment won't be in till
          Thursday.

Frank pushes his index finger against the plastic wrapping:
fossilized frosting cracks apart.

He finds an expiration date...

                    FRANK
          Best used by August 26th!

...and chucks the cupcake package at Chris, who ducks.

                    CHRIS
          Watch it! That junk is full of
          hydro-generated fats anyway. Eat a
          banana.

                    FRANK
          Can't, weird texture.

He tongs up the last surviving, severely wrinkled hot dog.
Then begins adding ketchup, mustard, and relish.

                    CHRIS
          So... you gonna spill the beans or
          what?

                    FRANK
          One of my staff had a supernatural
          encounter in the bathroom.

                    CHRIS
          Holy crap!

                    FRANK
          I know. Let's go.

Chris bounds over to the soda fountain area.

Frank positions his cup under the coffee dispenser.

                    FRANK
          How old is this?

Chris glances back, shrugs.

Ice chunks clatter into a "Bladder Buster Super Gulp."

Jenny replenishes sugar packets near Frank.

                    JENNY
          I made a fresh brew about ten
          minutes ago.

                    FRANK
          You're the best.

He pulls the lever.

                    JENNY
          Glad someone here thinks so.

Chris rolls his eyes as he hops between the eight carbonated
taps: performing his systematic ritual.

                    FRANK
          Does that disgusting concoction of
          yours ever taste the same?

                    CHRIS
          There's a science to making the
          perfect suicide.

He sips his creation, satisfied, snaps a lid on the bubbly
elixir.

Drinks in hand, the guys proceed out.

                    FRANK
          Good night, Jenny.

                    CHRIS
          If anyone asks, I'm dutifully
          stocking the freezer.

                    JENNY
          Stop right there, Christopher!

Chris hesitates at the entry.

Jenny stands behind the counter: phone in hand.

> CHRIS
> Calling out for pizza?

> JENNY
> Don't make me dial Rich. You can't
> afford another strike.

> CHRIS
> You wouldn't.

> JENNY
> Wouldn't I? Try me.

> CHRIS
> I don't think so. Why else are you
> volunteering to work my night
> shifts?

Chris vacates. Jenny looks defeated, conflicted.

> JENNY
> CHRISTOPHER!

EXT. GAS N GRUB

Chris raps on the Sunbird's rusting roof.

> CHRIS
> Here's a little nugget of advice.
> Never date --

> FRANK
> Exact warning I gave four months
> ago. But just between us, she's too
> good for you.

He dips from view.

> CHRIS
> Wait a minute.

EXT. SERVICE CENTER - NIGHT

Shouldering a backpack, Frank pushes the security box button.

He signals through the glass to TRAVIS, 30s, a security guard short in stature and clarity.

> FRANK
> Let me do the talking.

Chris sucks on his straw.

BUZZ. The entrance opens.

INT. SERVICE CENTER - SECURITY COUNTER

Travis rolls his key ring collection several times like it was a six-shooter.

>   TRAVIS
>   Evening, Frank. What's brought you
>   back at such a late hour?

>   FRANK
>   The bathroom. Chris has to go,
>   small bladder. Have you noticed
>   anything strange tonight?

>   TRAVIS
>   One time I fixed my brother's
>   toilet. He just got married and
>   moved to Virginia cause he's a
>   fighter pilot.

>   FRANK
>   So, uh, Cyrus wanted you to
>   understand, no one is to know we
>   stopped in -- not even Cyrus.

>   TRAVIS
>   Sure thing, Frank. One time I
>   panicked when my Mom didn't buy any
>   Butter Brickle ice cream. Brickle's
>   a funny word.

>   FRANK
>   Chris won't need a badge.

>   TRAVIS
>   (disturbing wink)
>   Noted. I mean *not* noted.

INT. SERVICE CENTER - BATHROOM - CAMCORDER POV

A red light and "REC" displays in the upper right corner. Wind chimes come into focus.

>   FRANK (O.S.)
>   Wind chimes hung.

Camcorder POV pans down to the floor.

>   FRANK (O.S.)
>   Flour spread.

Zooms in on the sink ledge where a grinning BOBBLEHEAD
MESSIAH sits.

Frank sets down the camcorder.

> FRANK
> Why's Bobblehead Messiah off my
> dash?

> CHRIS
> We need all the help we can get,
> even from religious novelties.

He flicks the head.

> CHRIS
> What better place for BM?

INT. SERVICE CENTER - BATHROOM - LATER

SUPERIMPOSE: "October 21 - 2:20 AM"

Frank lounges on the tile floor. Chris whizzes in a urinal.

> CHRIS
> Harold's ancient. He probably
> experienced hot flashes while on
> the can. Some kind of man-o-pause.

> FRANK
> He seemed spooked to me.
> *(thinks)*
> I remember Mr. Farkle liked to
> whistle.

> CHRIS
> Who?

He washes, then situates against the sink.

> FRANK
> Our former janitor. Died six months
> ago. Sweet old man. Used to say,
> "Farkle makes it sparkle."

The wind chimes jingle.

Frank fumbles the camcorder on.

Unnoticed, a greenish ORB pushes a faucet on before
disappearing.

                    CHRIS
              (*vaults off sink*)
         Look out!

Frank holds steady on the water.

                    FRANK
         Did you bump the handle?

                    CHRIS
         No way, something is definitely
         here.

A second faucet twists as the green Orb reappears...

                    CHRIS
         There it is! A floating gob.

                    FRANK
         Orb!

...and vanishes again.

Chris sticks his face in the camcorder.

                    CHRIS
         Did everyone see that? Visual
         confirmation, folks!

Wheels on the janitor's mop bucket squeak forward.

A glowing, sea-green pearlescent shape materializes into the
torso of a whistling old man. This is FARKLE'S GHOST.

Their jaws drop.

                    FRANK
              (*shocked*)
         A full-bodied apparition.

Frank trains the camcorder on Farkle's Ghost who mops like he
still had a pulse.

Chris panics, pats his pockets, realizes.

                    CHRIS
         Uh, Frank. I'm not sure how to say
         this, but I left the Kodak in your
         car.

                    FRANK
         Again? Use the Polaroid.

Chris readies the Polaroid camera.

                    CHRIS
          Excuse me. Mr. Farkle? Ghost
          janitor.

                    FRANK
          What are you doing?

                    CHRIS
          I want him to turn.

                    FRANK
          Just take the picture.

Chris frames his shot... BA-DUP. A Polaroid photo ejects from
the bottom and glides right under --

Farkle's Ghost. He pauses, looks back.

No one moves.

The apparition resumes working. His ethereal glow pulsates
while sopping the photo in dirty water.

                    FRANK
          Effort well wasted.

Chris ejects the cartridge.

                    CHRIS
          And the last of our film. What's
          next?

                    FRANK
          I think you know.

Chris sighs, hands Frank the camera. Performs his Sign of the
Cross.

He pops off the Bladder Buster lid and inches up behind
Farkle's Ghost.

Chris whistles, tips his cup over: soda splatters the floor.

Farkle's Ghost mops it up methodically, not paying him any
attention.

More soda splashes out. Farkle ponders the new spill then
stares at Chris.

                    CHRIS
          Frank? What's he doing?

                    FRANK
          No idea, stay on target.

Farkle's Ghost changes color, like a mood ring, to black opal.

                    CHRIS
          Frank...

His mouth stretches down -- low enough to swallow Chris's head -- and ROARS.

Chris screams! He splashes rest of his soda in Farkle's face. Dives into the nearest stall.

The iridescent specter hovers past, loops around, and charges!

                    FRANK
               (backing away)
          Hold on, Mr. Farkle. It's me!

Farkle slimes Frank as he passes through him and into the wall: leaving a syrupy goo imprint.

Chris pokes his head out, then rest of his body.

                    CHRIS
          That was friggin' bonkers! Oh, is
          the camera okay?

Frank wipes down the camcorder with a wad of paper towels.

                    FRANK
          You have a rare talent to annoy the
          dead as much as the living.

                    CHRIS
          At least I'm not biased.

Pipes RATTLE and MOAN. Chris ducks back into hiding.

Toilet water explodes within each stall.

                    FRANK
          Get out, Chris!

Chris YELPS. The door opens. He's drenched.

INT. SERVICE CENTER

Chris squishes behind Frank as they pass a sleeping Travis.

INT. APT - DAY

Frank relaxes on the couch.

                    FRANK
          Cyrus questioned me for thirty
          minutes about the mess.

Chris rummages the kitchen cupboards in his robe. Ignoring or
too focused to answer.

                    CHRIS
          That's nice.

                    FRANK
          Then Travis trapped me in a debate
          with himself on why waterpiks are
          superior to floss.

KNOCK-KNOCK-KNOCK.

Chris answers the door. Brooke holds several take-out bags.

                    CHRIS
          Hi, beautiful. Miss me?

She sidesteps him.

                    BROOKE
          You boys hungry?

Sets out an assortment of Chinese food on the bar.

                    BROOKE
          I wasn't sure what you liked, so I
          brought a little of everything.

                    CHRIS
               (fills a plate)
          Don't let this one go, Frank. She's
          a keeper.

He plops down in front of the TV.

Frank embraces Brooke.

                    FRANK
          You didn't need to do this.

                    BROOKE
          I wanted to. Plus, got us a Tales
          from the Crypt. Is Chris working
          tonight?

                    FRANK
          Most likely.

Brooke breaks free and retrieves the VHS cassette.

54.

                    FRANK
          Demon Knight. You're such an angel.
          Wait right here.

He disappears into his bedroom... returns with a Video8 tape
sealed in a Ziploc bag.

                    BROOKE
          Another so soon?

                    FRANK
          This isn't just another tape, it's
          the tape.

                    CHRIS
          The holy grail. Our ticket to green
          pastures of money!

                    BROOKE
          Better than the middle school?

                    FRANK
          Indisputable visual proof the
          paranormal exist among us.

                    BROOKE
          Awe-some! Can we watch it now?

                    CHRIS
          After my show's over.

Brooke's confused.

                    FRANK
          Pinky and the Brain. He records
          them.

                    BROOKE
          I see.

Frank hands her the tape...

                    FRANK
          It's our only copy.

...but has trouble letting go. She wrestles it from his grip.

                    BROOKE
          Don't worry. I'll keep it safe.

Brooke places it on her purse and heads to the kitchen sink.

She feverishly scrubs as Frank plays with a pair of
chopsticks.

                    FRANK
          Grandma's gonna miss you at the
          dinner table.

                    BROOKE
          She understands I'm a woman in
          demand.

                    FRANK
          In what way, exactly?

Brooke flicks water at him.

INT. VICTORIAN MANOR - BEDROOM - NIGHT

Morma shuffles past a large painting of two people camping on
the Swedish countryside.

She crawls under a thick comforter. Fits her reading glasses
on and opens a romance novel.

The nightstand lamp and ceiling lights flicker. A GUTTURAL
VOICE emanates from the walls.

She sets the book down.

                    MORMA   SUBTITLE
          Hello? Vem är det?   Who is there?

No answer, she resumes reading.

SMOKE billows from the painted fire. The Shadow Mist looms
over Morma.

She hustles out of bed. Pulls and twists the doorknob: it
doesn't budge.

                    MORMA
          Johan! Spöke!

Her ceiling light intensifies...

                    MORMA
          Johan! Johan!

...then bursts as the Shadow Mist engulfs her.

Pitch black. The door opens. Morma falls into Johan's arms,
terrified, babbling in Swedish.

                    JOHAN
          Mamma, Mamma, I'm here. Shhh,
          everything's okay.

She shakes her head.

                    MORMA
          Spöke, spöke.

Johan flips the light switch up and down.

          JOHAN   SUBTITLE
No mamma, it's only the   Old house.
wiring. Gammalt hus.

INT. PUBLIC ACCESS TV - MORNING

Brooke breezes in like a ray of sunshine. Sets one foot into
her room when --

                    LIAM (O.S.)
          Brooke, love.

The storm clouds roll in. She faces Liam.

                    BROOKE
             (curt)
          Yes, Liam?

                    LIAM
          I need you to make a highlight reel
          for Glenda.

                    BROOKE
          No way. I'm not wasting my time
          staring at her ta-tas. My day is
          booked.

                    LIAM
          Doing what?

                    BROOKE
          Mechanic Mike's promo, a meeting
          with Kitty, and editing fantastic
          new footage from Frank.

                    LIAM
          More bloody hours of dust balls.

                    BROOKE
          Irrefutable evidence of ghosts. And
          I don't appreciate your tone.

                    LIAM
          Bollocks.

>   BROOKE
> The truth will be known soon
> enough. Imagine Kitty's reaction
> when she learns it.

EXT. VICTORIAN MANOR - NIGHT

The Sunbird squeaks to a stop.

INT./EXT. SUNBIRD

Frank stares slack-jawed through the windshield.

Brook knocks on the driver-side window: he jumps. She opens his door.

EXT. VICTORIAN MANOR

As Frank steps out, Brook peppers him with kisses.

The mansion appears to loom over them. He staggers back.

>   BROOKE
> What's wrong? You're white as a
> ghost.

>   FRANK
> H-how long have you lived here?

>   BROOKE
> Since starting with Channel 14.

>   FRANK
> You haven't seen anything unusual?

She tugs on his arm, he resists.

>   BROOKE
> Don't be nervous. No one's going to
> bite.

INT. VICTORIAN MANOR - FOYER

Frank fidgets, afraid to touch anything. Nadine prances in.

>   NADINE
> I thought I heard someone.

>   BROOKE
> Mom, I'd like you to meet Frank.

>   NADINE
> How nice that you could join us.
> Brooke has told me so many stories.

                    BROOKE
          Mother...

                    NADINE
          I'm teasing.

                    FRANK
          You have a beautiful home, Mrs.
          Hallstrom.

                    NADINE
          Please, call me Nadine. I save
          "Mrs." for school conferences and
          her father's work functions -- who
          should be home any minute. Brooke,
          why not give Frank a tour?

She bustles off.

                    BROOKE
          Always the consummate hostess.

Brooke guides them to a designer wooden-leg sofa in the
LIVING ROOM.

                    FRANK
          Has Kitty seen our tape?

                    BROOKE
          Not yet. She waits until a show
          airs. Yours will be this Monday.

                    FRANK
          Great.

He fixates on a familiar oil lamp, hesitant to touch.

                    BROOKE
          One of several items my parents
          inherited with the house. Mom likes
          to light them on special occasions.

                    FRANK
          I'm not seeing any flame.

                    BROOKE
               (giggles)
          It's a long and arduous road to
          reach oil burning status. Be glad
          too, the fumes reek.

                    FRANK
          I'm surprised it works.

                    BROOKE
          They found one busted on the floor
          when moving in, but the rest are
          fine.

                    FRANK
          No kidding.

INT. VICTORIAN MANOR - DINING ROOM

Typical dinner interaction. Johan sits opposite Frank who
only musters a few bites of food. His eyes continually dart
around the room.

                    JOHAN
          So, Frank, Brooke tells me things
          are happening with the ghost show.

                    FRANK
          We hope so.

                    JOHAN
          You're serious about this venture.

                    FRANK
          Researching the paranormal is my
          life.

                    JOHAN
          I find difficulty believing there's
          any future with the dead.

                    BROOKE
          Undertakers might disagree.

Bobby snorts.

                    NADINE
          That's quite enough, Johan. You're
          making our guest uncomfortable.

                    JOHAN
          My apologies. I'm simply curious to
          learn what caused --

BADDDDONG is heard from a distant room.

                    JOHAN
          Please excuse me, I'll be right
          back.

Johan enters their immaculate STUDY and lifts a candlestick
receiver off an antique phone's cradle.

60.

                         JOHAN
                Hallstrom residence, Johan
                speaking.

The Shadow Mist seeps out of perforated holes into his ear.

Johan has a body shiver. He sets the receiver down. Studies
his fingers: wiggles them.

Johan returns to the DINING ROOM with a mischievous sneer on
his face.

                         JOHAN
                Welcome back, Frank. Long time, no
                see. All grown up.

His voice has changed: no accent, almost sinister.

                         FRANK
                    (nervous laugh)
                It's only been a few minutes.

                         JOHAN
                To some a few minutes can feel like
                an eternity, or at least thirteen
                years.

Frank becomes unnerved by Johan's piercing gaze.

                         MORMA
                Spöke!

            JOHAN   SUBTITLE
Stäng munnen innan jag skär   Close your mouth before I cut
ut tungan!   out your tongue!

She shrinks back in silence.

                         BROOKE
                Is everything okay, Daddy?

                         JOHAN
                Never better. I feel like a new
                man; though disappointed the son
                wasn't older.

                         BOBBY
                    (huffy)
                What'd I do now?

Johan ignores him, concentrates on the table's spread.

                    JOHAN
          Look at this succulent feast. I
          sure have missed eating.

He disregards etiquette and devours handfuls of food:
reaching from other plates.

Everyone gawks in disbelief.

Johan pauses, swallows, explodes in anger.

                    JOHAN
          It's rude to stare!

Nadine jumps in her seat.

                    NADINE
          Johan! What has gotten into you?

Johan regains his composure.

                    JOHAN
          This body needs rest.

He pushes his chair back.

Johan clenches Frank's shoulder before leaving.

                    JOHAN
          Don't run off again. We haven't
          finished.

Frank looks to an equally bewildered Brooke.

                    FRANK
          Finished what?

EXT. VICTORIAN MANOR

Brooke escorts Frank out.

                    BROOKE
          Sorry about my Dad. He was acting
          really odd tonight. I hope he
          didn't scare you off.

                    FRANK
          Do I look scared?

                    BROOKE
          A little.

He gets close, but she turns her head.

                         BROOKE
               I haven't brushed.

                         FRANK
               I'll risk it.

He folds her into his arms. They kiss. Frank peeks back at
the mansion and gasps.

Johan peers down from an upper window.

EXT. LIBRARY - NIGHT

A century old, stone structure.

INT. LIBRARY - ARCHIVES

Frank sits alone at a row of microfiche viewers flanked by
file cabinets.

Newspaper articles flicker past his face.

He cranks back a dial, stops, then slowly advances until he
sees ON THE SCREEN:

          "MASSACRE AT FARRINGTON HOME -- November 25, 1952

               A city mourns over the shocking loss of
               Dr. Farrington and his family. A pillar of
               this community, police are baffled to why an
               apparent murder/suicide was committed by
               Farrington's eldest son..."

INT. VICTORIAN MANOR - DAY - FLASHBACK (BLACK & WHITE)

Boots clunk down a staircase.

THREE GENERATIONS are gathered around the dining room table.

DR. FARRINGTON, 60s, stern face, rises. Rest of the family
recoil in fear.

His SON, 41, raises a rifle, grins.

A series of muzzle flashes.

Blood pools beneath the table, seeping through the floor
boards.

The Son jams the gun under his chin.

                         SON
               This was fun.

His finger squeezes the trigger. A high-pitched RINGING --

INT. FRANK'S BEDROOM - DAY (1997)

-- alters into an irritating alarm BEEP. A groggy Frank
flounders a hand to the nightstand and presses various
buttons until silent.

The blurry, cockeyed Zuul clock comes into focus: 8:35.

INT. APT - LATER

Frank bumbles out of the apartment in a half-dressed state.

Creepers watches from his usual spot: next to an empty bowl.
He meows.

In the HALLWAY, muffled, repetitive MEOWING permeates through
the apartment door.

EXT. SERVICE CENTER - DAY

Chris jogs up to the side entrance crowded by SMOKERS.

> CHRIS
> Excuse me, clean lungs coming
> through. Please blow your cancer
> the other direction.

He receives several dirty looks. FUNKY HAIR blows a cloud in
his face.

> FUNKY HAIR
> Oops.

Chris coughs, waves away the smoke.

> CHRIS
> I could sue you for a health
> assault.

> FUNKY HAIR
> Pfft.

Funky Hair flicks his cigarette ashes.

Chris waits...

> CHRIS
> You gonna badge me in or what?

INT. SERVICE CENTER

Frank raps his fingers on the desk, phone to ear. He glances at his desk clock.

> FRANK
> Yes, ma'am. I understand. Everyone forgets. No, he shouldn't have called you that.

He rolls his eyes.

Chris drum rolls the top of Frank's wall.

> FRANK
> *(fast)*
> After careful review you've been awarded a ten day extension. Goodbye.

Frank and Chris weave through the rows...

> FRANK
> What are you doing here?

> CHRIS
> Our big premiere. History in the making. Where else would I be when Lancaster county citizens finally see how extra-ordinary I am. Will there be any place to sit?

... and enter the BREAK ROOM. The doors squeak shut.

> FRANK
> I see a few open spots.

Not a living soul but for Vikram, and Quinn who greets them.

> QUINN
> Okay, what gives? Why's Chris here?

> FRANK
> To meet the fan club.

Quinn bear hugs Chris.

> QUINN
> Hey, buddy. Name's Quinn. It's a real honor.

Chris grunts as his rib cage becomes compressed.

                    CHRIS
          Pleased - to meet - you.

Quinn releases him.

                    CHRIS
          Today's episode will be nothing
          like you've seen before. It's like
          Spooked, squared.

They sit as the low-budget Spooked title sequence plays --
becomes garbled -- goes black.

                    CHRIS
          What the hell's going on?

                    FRANK
          This set has always been flaky.

                    QUINN
          Should bounce back any second. See.

ON THE TV: A dated black & white "Please Stand By" title card
appears. Liam walks out in front.

                    LIAM
          We're sorry but due to technical
          difficulties this episode of
          Spooked will never be seen... by
          anyone... ever. Cheerio.

INT. PUBLIC ACCESS TV - DAY

Frank rushes inside with Chris on his heels.

                    FRANK
          Brooke! Brooke!

                    CHRIS
          Sharon!

It takes them a moment to realize the place is deserted.

                    CHRIS
          Anyone?

                    FRANK
          Liam!

He looks down the HALLWAY at Liam, squaring off like an Old
West showdown with a Video8 tape in one hand; metal pan and
can of lighter fluid at his feet.

66.

                    LIAM
          They're gone, Frank. Out at
          Miller's Pumpkin Farm. Today's the
          annual "Squash Out Hunger" food
          drive.

                    FRANK
          What happened to our show!?

                    LIAM
          Technical difficulties. The tape
          was horribly mangled in playback.
          An unfortunate accident, but I
          warned Sharon this would happen on
          our relic of a machine.

                    CHRIS
               (whispers to Frank)
          Looks fine to me.

Liam flips it in the air.

                    CHRIS
          Careful! You've any idea how
          important that tape is in
          fulfilling my dream of big money
          and easy women?

                    LIAM
          We wouldn't be standing here if I
          didn't, you twit.

                    CHRIS
          Yeah, well Bowie's a freak!

                    LIAM
               (livid)
          Shut your cakehole, prat!

Frank gives a "WTF" face to Chris who shrugs.

                    FRANK
          Just take it easy, Liam. Let's not
          do anything rash.

                    LIAM
          Glenda's my ticket out of this two-
          bit operation. She makes it big, so
          will I.

He snaps the tape cover off.
                    FRANK
          Wait!

Frank goes into shock as --

Liam rips several feet of film out, drops it in the pan, and douses the cassette.

> CHRIS
> Nooooo!

Liam flips open his "Ziggy Stardust" lighter. Ignites the cartridge into a flaming dish.

Chris's knees buckle. He reaches out to the burning plastic.

The exposed film crinkles and shrinks. Noxious, black smoke rises.

> LIAM
> The sweet smell of success.

Frank looks at his tape, then Liam's smug expression. WHACK!

He's on the ground. Liam staggers up, covering his cheek: gauges Frank's exit.

> LIAM
> Ya bloody well sealed your fate,
> Peril! Expect to hear from my
> lawyer, the coppers, and your
> mother.

The fumes reach a sprinkler head.

Water showers upon him.

INT. APT - LATER

Frank lumbers in.

> FRANK
> There's nothing we can do. The
> little prick won.

Chris mopes behind, notices a strange document on the floor.

> CHRIS
> It's not the end of the world.

Frank opens the fridge and retrieves a Hi-C "Ecto Cooler" juice box -- 1 of 30 stacked on the top shelf.

> FRANK
> Delusional boy, we don't get
> another shot at Farkle.

                    CHRIS
          So we find a new water cooler
          worthy, supernatural phenomenon.

He leans on the kitchen bar, holding the document.

                    FRANK
          In a week? Have better luck filming
          you covered in flour with Vaseline
          smeared on the lens.

Frank pulls a package of peas from the freezer and sets it on
his knuckles.

                    CHRIS
          I'm not against the idea. How's the
          hand?

                    FRANK
          Painful.

Chris skims the fine print.

                    CHRIS
          Jesus, Mary, and Joseph, Frank;
          we're being evicted!

Frank snatches the eviction notice from him. Straw in mouth,
he reads as the Hi-C box crumples.

                    FRANK
          Pet ordinance violation? Damn it!
          How did they -- CREEPERS!

Creepers bolts from under the couch.

Frank crumples up the paper with his bruised hand.

                    FRANK
          Fate has spoken.

He flings it back at Chris; storms off.

                    FRANK (O.S.)
          Now the world has ended!

                                              TO BLACK.

BURRING.

                    CHRIS (O.S.)
          Hello? He's indisposed. Still.

SUPERIMPOSE: "October 30"

EXT./INT. APT - FRANK'S BEDROOM - DAY

Chris hangs up the phone.

> CHRIS
> Douchebag.

He knocks, tries the handle: locked. Smacks the door.

> CHRIS
> Frank!

Frank snaps his head up. Dazed. Remnants of a sugar bender gone bad. His floor littered with used juice boxes and junk food wrappers.

> FRANK
> What?

He face plants the pillow.

> CHRIS
> Cyrus called again. Sounded more
> peeved than usual.

No reply. Chris presses his ear to the door.

> CHRIS
> C'mon, Frank. This constant moping
> doesn't help anyone.

> FRANK
> (muffled)
> Don't care, go away.

> CHRIS
> I know the job sucks, but putting
> fired with evicted gets you
> homeless. And we can't hunt ghosts
> from a poorly construed cardboard
> box, pissing in the gutter -- which
> still trumps moving back in with my
> parents!

INT. PUBLIC ACCESS TV

Carolina waves as Chris passes through a busy reception.

Glenda sashays out of Kitty's room in a business executive outfit.

> CHRIS
> Glenda?

                    GLENDA
          Hi there, Chris-ta-pher.

                    CHRIS
          I barely recognized you so...
          dressed.

                    GLENDA
          The suit was Roger's idea. He
          thought it'd help my meeting with
          Kitty. Took me all morning to find
          one that fit over the girls.

She unbuttons the jacket, stretches.

                    CHRIS
          Ah, yes, I see how that would be a,
          um, problem. New look for the show?

                    GLENDA
          Not in the garden. I only wear my
          bibs. Imagine what a mess I'd be
          without them.

Chris retreats to his happy place.

                    CHRIS
          I have... way to often.

Glenda leans forward and kisses him on the cheek.

                    GLENDA
          Don't ever change.

Brooke watches Glenda leave with a look of disapproval but
quickly becomes sympathetic.

                    BROOKE
          I'm so sorry, Chris. I heard what
          happened. Is Frank mad at me?

                    CHRIS
          Just Liam, but I've never seen him
          in such a funk. Maybe you could
          swing by.

                    BROOKE
          Does he need a little TLC?

                    CHRIS
          Yes. As much as the current
          intimacy level allows.

> BROOKE
> I'll keep that in mind.

> CHRIS
> Wait a minute. What exactly did you
> hear?

INT. SERVICE CENTER - CYRUS'S OFFICE - DAY

Cyrus stares at Frank's bloodshot, unshaven visage.

> CYRUS
> Three days. Three days gone and no
> explanation. That alone is grounds
> for termination.

Frank remains silent, vacant.

> CYRUS
> But I'm a man of second chances.

Frank becomes more sullen.

> CYRUS
> Three months suspension. You'll
> help Sadie's group catch up on
> their loan apps. Move to the empty
> cube outside my office.

INT. APT - SAME

The lock clicks. Brooke enters, vamped up. She wears a mid-length trench coat and high heels.

> BROOKE
> Anyone home?

She flattens out the eviction notice.

> BROOKE
> (concerned)
> Frank?

Brooke enters FRANK'S BEDROOM. She covers her nose and throws open the nearest window. Surveys the squalor.

Creeper purrs, rubs against her leg. She pets him. Picks up a dirty sock by the very tips of her fingers.

> BROOKE
> Poor kitty. How do you live with
> him?

Slips off her high heels.

72.

INT. APT - FRANK'S BEDROOM - LATER

Cleaned. Dusted. Spotless. Brooke lays on the bed in her form-fitting Ghostbusters costume: zipper low enough to reveal cleavage.

Creepers, resting near her, perks up.

Frank lumbers in.

                    BROOKE
          Hi, stranger.

                    FRANK
          Brooke -- wow. Wow!

                    BROOKE
          Is that for me or the cleaning?

He forms a goofy grin.

                    FRANK
          Yes.

Brooke gets up, rounds the bed.

                    BROOKE
          I couldn't believe how pungent this
          room smelled. Are you protesting
          the eviction by not showering?

She waves the wrinkled paper.

                    FRANK
              (smells shirt)
          I've showered.

Brooke pushes him to the bed, straddles his lap. She uncaps the Binaca: double spritz in the mouth, then several sweeps across his chest.

                    BROOKE
          Chris enlightened me about the Liam
          altercation. Want to talk about it?

                    FRANK
          Not really.

Brooke removes her glasses, lays on Frank's chest, and coos into his ear.

                    BROOKE
          He also said, I should cheer you
          up.

She kisses his neck, then returns upright and draws the
zipper down to her navel.

The costume falls off. Brooke reaches behind, unhooks her
lace bra.

EXT. GAS N GRUB - DAY

Chris tips the lid off a waste basket as a white panel van
pulls up to the gas pump.

He struggles at removing the garbage sack.

The driver's side opens. Quinn jumps out.

> QUINN
> Chris.

> CHRIS
> Here to abduct me?

> QUINN
> Help you.

Quinn lifts the bag out with one hand.

> CHRIS
> I would've gotten it, eventually.

INT. APT - FRANK'S BEDROOM - LATER

Brooke snuggles between Frank's arms, draped in his t-shirt
like a nightie.

> BROOKE
> Creepers could live with me.

> FRANK
> Just Creepers?

> BROOKE
> I don't think we're there quite
> yet. At least not while under my
> father's roof.

> FRANK
> How is dear old Dad?

> BROOKE
> Bizarre. Hasn't been to work since
> the night you visited.

> FRANK
> Mid-life crisis?

                    BROOKE
          Sabbatical, supposedly. Taking a
          vacation from himself -- his words.
          Every day he dresses like Paul
          Bunyan.

                    FRANK
          Must be having Halloween early.

                    BROOKE
          I don't understand why he needs an
          axe. Oh, almost forgot.

She fishes out a package of Hostess Cupcakes from her purse.

                    BROOKE
          My other surprise.

Frank's eyes widen.

He opens one side. Slides the confection halfway out.
Lightly presses on the vanilla squiggles.

The icing top stays in tact like only soft cupcakes can.

He whiffs the cocoa aroma.

                    FRANK
          They're so fresh. How did you --

                    BROOKE
          A girl has her ways.

Frank savors his first taste of chocolate heaven.

                    FRANK
          Mmmm.

He takes another bite: pure ecstasy.

                    BROOKE
          Should I give you and the cupcake
          some privacy?

Brooke puts her glasses back on.

                    FRANK
          Sorry, I haven't had one this moist
          in a long time.

                    BROOKE
          Sounds perverted.

                         FRANK
              Here, have a bite.

She slinks back from the offer.

                         BROOKE
              I'll pass. It's your treat.

Frank considers... passes her the other protected cupcake.

                         FRANK
              Such cake confection perfection
              deserves to be enjoyed by someone
              just as sweet.

                         BROOKE
                    (sly look)
              If I didn't know any better.

She tips the cupcake out and sinks her teeth into the
frosting.

                         BROOKE
              Yummy.

                         FRANK
              See. And you barely touched the
              creamy filling.

                         BROOKE
              Like this?

Brooke peers over her glasses.

Sticks her tongue into the cupcake center and rolls out the
frosting when --

Chris barges in. Huffing. Out of breath.

                         CHRIS
              Ran... all the way... here.

Brooke licks her lips.

                         BROOKE
              From the Gas N Grub?

                         CHRIS
                    (gulps air)
              Bus stop. Am I interrupting?

                         BROOKE
              Just dessert.

                              FRANK
                    Next time try --

                              CHRIS
                    Knocking first. Yes. Good call. But
                    this can't wait.

EXT. QUINN'S HOUSE - DAY

A quaint one-story single dwelling with the same white panel
van in the driveway.

INT. QUINN'S HOUSE

A 36" CRT TV and LaserDisc media center take prominence in an
otherwise modest residence.

Quinn holds Brooke's hand in a warm gesture.

                              QUINN
                    I don't believe I've had the
                    pleasure. Name's Quinn.

She politely withdraws it.

                              BROOKE
                    Brooke.

Quinn gives her the once-over.

                              QUINN
                    Were you at a costume party?

                              BROOKE
                         (slight blush)
                    Something like that.

He pats Frank's shoulder.

                              QUINN
                    Thanks for stopping by. Can I get
                    anyone a lemonade or Fresca?

                              FRANK
                    Chris insisted. Said you had stuff
                    here that would blow my mind.

Chris manipulates a multi-colored remote. A crisp, widescreen
image of "Poltergeist" plays on the TV.

                              CHRIS
                    Check it out. LASERDISC.

Brooke scoffs at his excitement.

                    BROOKE
          I'm so glad we rushed over.

                    QUINN
          He wasn't talking about this.

                    CHRIS
          Yeah, I mean, not only.

INT. QUINN'S HOUSE - SPARE ROOM

A modified workshop. Tools, workbench, and several inventions
occupy the space. Frank's in awe.

He picks up a burlap sack shaped like a basketball with
fishing wire attached to a drawstring.

                    QUINN
          A flour bomb. Fill up the sack,
          throw it, and pull the line.

                    FRANK
          Could be useful.

                    BROOKE
          I know I shouldn't ask.

                    QUINN
          Used to quickly discombobulate any
          suspected specter.

                    CHRIS
          Does this fire particle beams?

Chris pretends shooting the handle of a painted PVC pipe. The
braided hose connects it to a hiker's backpack.

                    QUINN
          Only water for now. The storage
          vessel holds three gallons. With
          proper pressure it can shoot thirty
          feet out.

Quinn unzips the top. Chris raps the large metal cylinder.

                    CHRIS
          Have you tried any other liquids?

Frank inspects a modified WET/DRY VAC fitted with two   12-
volt car batteries. Attached insulated copper wire feeds into
the unit through drilled holes.

                    QUINN
          Here's my greatest triumph.

78.

                    FRANK
          I assume the added juice is for
          more than sucking up saw dust.

                    QUINN
          The copper wire wraps in opposite
          directions around two iron bars.
          When powered on, the opposing
          magnetic fields should make an
          impenetrable cage for any ghost
          sucked inside.

                    FRANK
          You made a Ghostbusters trap!

                    QUINN
          In theory. It's never been field
          tested.

                    CHRIS
          What'd you name this bad boy?
          Creature container, spirit
          suspender, wait -- vapor vacuum!

                    FRANK
          Would you have any interest in
          becoming an official member of
          Spooked?

                    BROOKE
          Does this mean...?

                    FRANK
          It's time we pay Mrs. Vine another
          visit.

                    CHRIS
          Yes! Spocked trifecta!

                    QUINN
          Believe me, I never planned for
          this to happen...

Quinn slides open the closet.

                    QUINN
          ...only the possibility.

Three custom FLIGHT SUITS hang inside.

Chris and Frank stare in weirded-out giddiness.

Quinn pulls out a suit stitched with Chris's name and
compares it next to him.

> QUINN
> I guessed your sizes. Plus, a
> little something extra.

He turns it around. Emblazoned on the back is the Spooked
logo.

> FRANK
> I'm not sure which disturbs me
> more: the suits, or that you sew.

> QUINN
> Got an A in Home Ec.

EXT. QUINN'S HOUSE

Suited up, all three strut towards the van. Frank holds a
flour bomb. Chris maneuvers the wet/dry vac. Quinn carries
everything else.

Brooke calls to them from the Mustang.

> BROOKE
> I'll meet you at the station after
> I go home and change. We can
> recruit TRC's camera crew.

> FRANK
> Good idea, but Brooke... save the
> outfit.

INT. PUBLIC ACCESS TV - DAY

Chris, Frank, and Quinn march in. Frank can't help himself.

> FRANK
> Anybody see a ghost?

Carolina claps and scoots out from behind her desk.

> CAROLINA
> Muy caliente! I've always loved a
> man in uniform.

She teases her fingers down Chris's sleeve.

> CHRIS
> At your service.

> CAROLINA
> Who's the new guy?

> FRANK
> Quinn. Our equipment specialist.

> QUINN
> *(smooth)*
> Belleza como la suya no debe estar oculto detrás de un teléfono.

> SUBTITLE
> Beauty like yours shouldn't be hidden behind a phone.

He kisses Carolina's hand.

> CAROLINA
> I like him.

> CHRIS
> *(to Quinn)*
> What'd you say?

Carolina trots back to her counter.

> CAROLINA
> Is all this for a Halloween special?

She reaches over for a call. Chris admires the view.

> CHRIS
> Yes, precisely. A Halloween episode to unveil our new look.

> FRANK
> We'll see what Brooke thinks first.

> LIAM
> She isn't here.

He approaches sporting a BRUISED CHEEK.

> CHRIS
> Wow, Liam, was Bowie recently punched out?

Liam scowls at Chris. Brandishes a document.

> LIAM
> Read it and weep.

> FRANK
> You're resignation letter?

> LIAM
> Letter of intent, for Glenda, from The Reality Channel management.

> CHRIS
> Bull nuts.

Kitty joins them.

                    LIAM
          Ah, Kitty love, enlighten Chris
          here on the art of negotiation.

                    KITTY
          I'd rather hear an explanation for
          this note Brooke left on my desk.

                    LIAM
          I don't know what you mean.

Kitty removes the Letter of Intent from his hands. He becomes
flustered as she rips the paper in half.

                    KITTY
          Allow me to enlighten you, Mr.
          Swindal. Please join Sharon in my
          office.

Liam grumbles off.

Carolina hangs up the phone.

                    CAROLINA
               (puzzled)
          That was Brooke's papa. He wants
          Frank to know: Ted waits for him.

Chris gives Frank the same alarmed expression.

                    CHRIS/FRANK
          Brooke's in trouble.

                    QUINN
          Who's Ted?

                    FRANK
          I'll explain on the way.

They hurry out.

                    KITTY
          Frank.

He pauses, turns.

                    KITTY
          How can I help?

82.

EXT. PUBLIC ACCESS TV - PARKING - VAN

Quinn slides open the panel door, but Chris doesn't board.
Frank catches up.

>   FRANK
>   What's the problem?

>   CHRIS
>   I've got an idea. Give me the
>   backpacks.

>   FRANK
>   There isn't time.

>   CHRIS
>   Trust me. If Ted's really back --
>   have I ever let you down?

Frank raises an eyebrow.

>   CHRIS
>   When it's important! Let's do this.

Quinn fastens the first pack to Chris who almost tips over.

Liquid SLOSHES as Quinn steadies him. Chris bear hugs the
other one.

>   QUINN
>   Are you good?

>   CHRIS
>   (grunts)
>   Fine. Go save Brooke.

>   FRANK
>   Make it quick. Don't let chivalry
>   die, or us.

Frank and Quinn climb inside. Chris lumbers towards the bus
stop.

EXT. VICTORIAN MANOR - DAY

The van parks along the curb. Quinn and Frank jump out of the
back.

>   QUINN
>   Sounds to me like Ted's a
>   poltergeist.

They unload the equipment.

                    FRANK
          He's something more... pure evil.
          Ever encounter a demonic entity?

Quinn shakes his head. Frank palms a flour bomb.

                    FRANK
          Be ready for anything.

An SUV for The Reality Channel pulls up behind them.

INT. METRO BUS - SAME

Chris jostles about in his seat as he cradles a backpack in
each arm. An OLD COUPLE stares from across the aisle.

INT. VICTORIAN MANOR

Quinn, Frank, and a CAMERA MAN stand in the foyer. The Camera
Man films everything.

                    CAMERA MAN
          Posh.

Frank does a double-take.

                    QUINN
          Where is everyone?

                    FRANK
          Brooke?

                    BROOKE (O.S.)
          Frank? Frank! We're in here!

                    BOBBY (O.S.)
          Help us!

INT. CHURCH

Chris rests the two backpacks near a holy water receptacle
and splashes his face.

                    CHRIS
          Father Nick! Come quick!

FATHER NICK, 53, lanky with robust compassion, hastens down
the aisle.

                    FATHER NICK
          Are you ready to confess, Chris? Is
          the weight of your sin such a heavy
          burden?

                    CHRIS
          No, just these canisters of pop. I
          need you to bless them.

                    FATHER NICK
          I'm not sure I understand.

                    CHRIS
          Gas N Grub only has filtered water,
          not holy. Bless my soda, Father,
          make it sacred.

                    FATHER NICK
          My son, the Church does not condone
          such requests.

Chris grabs Father Nick's shirt with both hands and pulls him
down to eye level.

                    CHRIS
          Lives are at risk, Father! My best
          friend's girlfriend's dad is
          possessed by a demon! We need to
          stop him before he does something
          real bad.

INT. VICTORIAN MANOR - LIVING ROOM

Frank and Quinn discover the Hallstrom family roped to dining
table chairs.

                    NADINE
          Thank goodness you're here.

                    BROOKE
          My dad has completely lost it.

                    BOBBY
          He's a whack-job!

                    NADINE
          Bobby! That's no way to talk.

                    BOBBY
          Are you kidding me?!

They ponder hopelessly over the intricate knot binding...

                    FRANK
          It's not really your father. I
          think he's possessed by a demon
          named Ted.

...make a vain attempt at freeing Brooke.

                    BROOKE
          Ted? From the Ouija board?

                    TED/JOHAN (O.S.)
          Not exactly.

INT. METRO BUS

Chris lugs his backpacks past many JUDGMENTAL EYES until he
finds an empty seat. He nods to the same Old Couple.

The OLD MAN points with a cane.

                    OLD MAN
          Look ma, the freak is back.

                    CHRIS
          Watch your mouth, pops. Waiting at
          death's doorstep won't stop me from
          knocking your teeth out, if you had
          any left.

INT. VICTORIAN MANOR - LIVING ROOM

THUMP-CLUNK, THUMP-CLUNK: work boots and an axe appear on the
staircase.

The Camera Man spins away from Frank's all-thumbs rescue and
sees --

Johan, the mountain man.

                    TED/JOHAN
          Ouija is like chum to a shark. I
          can't resist the lure when someone
          opens the doorway.

Bobby watches as the would-be rescuers desperately use sheer
strength to break his sister's bonds. No effect.

                    BOBBY
          We're dead.

                    TED/JOHAN
          It's been over two hundred years
          since I last tied such a knot.
          Haven't lost my touch.

Frank faces Johan with an authoritative facade.

                    FRANK
          L-leave this house now Ted, or face
          the consequences.

> TED/JOHAN
> Such big talk from a whelp.

Quinn stands between them.

> TED/JOHAN
> Who might this be? Chris?

> QUINN
> The consequence. I'm going to thump
> you back to the days of Sodom.

Johan muses at the foot of the stairs.

> TED/JOHAN
> Good times.
> *(points his axe)*
> Let's find out. I have all the time
> in the world and then some.

EXT. NEIGHBORHOOD

Chris trudges up the sidewalk, panting, bearing his front and
back packs. Sweat pours off his forehead.

> CHRIS
> Hang on, Frank. Almost there.

INT. VICTORIAN MANOR - LIVING ROOM

Quinn lunges his massive frame at Johan who swats him down
with supernatural strength. Johan raises the axe when --

A decorative pillow bumps his head. He turns, sees Frank
standing near the wooden-leg sofa. Throws the axe like a
tomahawk!

The blade embeds inches from Frank's head: into an
impressionist painting.

> NADINE
> Not the Monet!

Frank tugs at the handle but is flung back.

Johan rips the axe out of the wall. He advances.

Frank scuttles backward until pressed against the TV.

Johan hovers over him. Brings the axe down -- misjudges,
shattering the screen.

> BOBBY
> NOT THE TV!

Frank kicks Johan's leg out from under him and escapes.

Johan regains his footing.

                    TED/JOHAN
               (laughs)
          I'm impressed. There's a little
          fight in you after all.

His face forms a devilish grimace.

Little BULGES spread like wildfire under Frank's flight suit.

Frank wiggles about, performing a bizarre dance... finally
pulls down the zipper.

DOZENS OF SPIDERS scurry out and swarm him.

                    FRANK
          Get 'em off! Get 'em off!

Quinn locks his arms around Johan but gets tossed into the
air.

He crashes onto the wooden-leg sofa that buckles.

                    TED/JOHAN
          This is fun.

EXT. NEIGHBORHOOD

A faded '87 BMW Z1 Roadster VROOMS towards the

VICTORIAN MANOR

and stops inches from the SUV. Liam scrambles out, cuts past
the thick oak tree -- collides into Chris.

          LIAM   CHRIS
What are you doing?   What are you doing?

                    CHRIS
          Here.

They glare at each other. Liam brushes himself off. Chris
props up a pack.

                    CHRIS
          Be useful for once and find out.

Liam sneers, but takes it and heads into the manor.

                    CHRIS
          No, no, I got this.

He wobbles on his back like an overturned turtle.

INT. VICTORIAN MANOR - LIVING ROOM

Johan smashes Quinn against a wall while focused on Frank's torture.

Liam races in, drops the pack, and abruptly halts.

> LIAM
> I demand to know -- oh!

Johan takes notice.

The spiders instantly dissolve.

> TED/JOHAN
> (studies Liam)
> Aaah yes, I remember. The mouthy miscreant who wet himself. Back for another slapping?

> LIAM
> I, uh...

Chris staggers in and plops onto an upholstered chair.

> CHRIS
> I can't feel my legs.

> FRANK
> Don't sit now. Serve the suicide!

Chris wobbles to his feet. Aims the PVC pipe.

A jet of liquid shoots across the room, spattering Johan.

> TED/JOHAN
> (licks his lips)
> Not bad.

Quinn head butts Johan and wrestles him to the ground. Frank piles on top.

Their feeble effort soon languishes.

> FRANK
> Move it, Chris!

Chris teeters over.

> QUINN
> Flush his system.

He crams the sprayer tip down Johan's mouth.

                    CHRIS
          Bottoms up.

Soda ricochets everywhere from the high-pressure delivery.

Johan flails about, choking, unable to escape... then nothing. He lays motionless.

                    NADINE   BROOKE
Johan!   Daddy!

                    CHRIS
          Is he dead?

His body convulses in a full on seizure, mouth foaming. Soda gushes out like Old Faithful.

Ted surges from Johan's mouth in his shadow form with a deep GUTTURAL RUMBLE, covered in a syrupy mix.

A wet stain spreads over Liam's crotch.

                    FRANK
          Quinn, the trap!

Frank hurls a flour bomb and yanks the cord.

Flour explodes throughout the air, coating Ted into a traditional white ghost.

Flour particles disperse as the wet/dry vac hose makes contact. Ted's ghostly face shows genuine surprise.

Quinn winks.

A green LED lights up. Loud WHIRRING.

The powdery specter slurps down the hose.

Quinn inspects the trap, shakes it a little.

                    QUINN
          We got him.

Everybody cheers!

Frank uses the axe to saw through Brooke's rope. She jumps into his arms and peppers him with kisses.

                    NADINE
          Brooke... honey.

                    BOBBY
          Get me out of this!

Brooke checks on Johan while rest of the family are freed.

Johan opens his eyes and coughs. Puzzles over his outfit.

                    JOHAN
          Why am I the Marlboro man? And all
          sticky?

Brooke helps him up.

                    BROOKE
          Long story.

Nadine embraces him.

                    NADINE
          Johan, pookums, you're back.

Quinn, Chris, and Frank surround the wet/dry vac.

                    FRANK
          Never underestimate the power of
          bad tasting pop. Chris's suicide
          mix repulsed Ted better than
          expected.

                    CHRIS
          I had Father Nick bless the
          canisters.

                    QUINN
          Sacred soda? Smart thinking.

Chris beams.

A red LED blinks on the trap. Batteries fizzle. The wet/dry
vac RATTLES.

                    QUINN
          Oh no.

The top blows off.

Ted emerges bigger, darker, bits of sticky flour still
attached. He bellows words in Swedish, Hebrew, and Aramaic:

                    TED
          Your souls will writhe under
          Satan's heel for all eternity.

BLOOD seeps down the walls.

Oil lamps spout FLAMES.

Ted swoops after his frightened prey scattering for cover.

Chris thrusts his rosary at the demon who swats it from his hand.

The beads CLATTER unseen.

Ted clutches Frank by his neck and suspends him mid-air, REFLECTED in the Camera Man's lens.

                    BROOKE (O.S.)
          Frank!

Quinn and Chris take position. PVC guns primed at the hip.

Simultaneous streams of holy soda strike Ted who howls, releasing Frank.

He scurries to safety.

                    FRANK
          Perfect timing, again.

                    CHRIS
          We'll settle up later.

Ted agonizes from the relentless fizzy onslaught.

                    QUINN
          Woo-hoo! Now *this* is fun!

                    CHRIS
          How do we bring it home?

                    FRANK
          No idea.

One stream crosses into the other, holds...

Chris notices the other two staring.

                    CHRIS
          Worth a shot.

His gun tapers off.

                    CHRIS
          I'm out.

Quinn forces Ted into a corner: shadow body diminishing.

92.

                    QUINN
          Mine won't last much longer.

                    CHRIS
          That's it then. Find the jam, we're
          toast.

Frank reaches into his pocket.

                    FRANK
          Not yet.

He places Bobblehead Messiah in Chris's hand.

                    CHRIS
          Bobby M?

                    FRANK
          Even religious novelties can be
          compelling.

Chris nods, takes a resolute step forward. He shakes the
oversized head like a rattle.

                    CHRIS
               (trembles)
          In the name of Jesus Christ, our
          holy savior, Emmanuel --

Quinn's stream dribbles.

                    CHRIS
               (stronger)
          -- blessed redeemer and almighty
          Father.

The malevolent specter's smoky mass billows.

                    CHRIS
          I cast you back to the pits of
          hell!

He throws Bobblehead Messiah.

It sails through the air... serene face wobbling in
disapproval... and collides with Ted.

BOOM! The demonic entity explodes: rippling through the
mansion like a sound wave.

Lamps topple, the room ignites.

EXT. VICTORIAN MANOR - DUSK

Liam spearheads the escape to his car. Quinn follows, carrying out Morma.

The rest gather on the street.

Johan holds Nadine and his kids close. They watch as the fire consumes their home.

EXT. VICTORIAN MANOR - NIGHT

Neighbors look on as emergency vehicles light up the street amid the smoldering wreck.

Chris, Frank, and Kitty crowd near an ambulance. Johan comforts Morma as she receives oxygen on a stretcher.

> JOHAN
> I can't express how grateful I am.
> Whatever you need, just ask.

Frank preempts Chris by clenching his shoulder.

> FRANK
> Chris and I couldn't be happier
> having experienced such an
> incredible ordeal. Right?

Chris nods in silent submission.

> KITTY
> A decision hasn't been finalized
> for the new show. "Glenda's Garden"
> was under consideration.

> JOHAN
> Maybe for Showtime. No, I think
> "Spooked" could be a more...
> inspired addition; if they're
> interested.

> CHRIS
> I LOVE YOU!

He embraces Johan.

> JOHAN
> A yes is sufficient.

Frank jerks him back.

> FRANK
> How can you make that decision?

                    KITTY
          He's the CEO. I'll draw up the
          contracts.

PARAMEDICS check on Morma and remove her oxygen mask. They
help Johan stand her up.

                    JOHAN
          It's been a long night. We'll talk
          more next week.

He ushers Morma to an idling Mercedes-Benz Sedan.

Kitty shakes Frank's hand.

                    KITTY
          Congratulations, gentleman. I'll
          send you a copy of our footage
          after it's processed.

                    FRANK
          No rush.

                    CHRIS
          You'll need time to take in all of
          my extra-ordinariness.

EXT. VICTORIAN MANOR - DAY

SUPERIMPOSE: "6 Months Later"

Construction site. Workers are distributed across a grand
skeletal structure.

Johan consults a blueprint. Hands cover his eyes.

                    BROOKE (O.S.)
          Guess who?

He turns, smiles.

                    JOHAN
          Hello, honey. Frank.

                    FRANK
          The framing looks very impressive,
          Mr. Hallstrom.

                    JOHAN
          It really does. This crew has been
          working at breakneck speed.

He grabs Frank's shoulder.

                    JOHAN
          But please, Frank, enough with the
          formality. Call me Johan, or John,
          or Dad.

                    BROOKE
          Daddy...

The FOREMAN gestures Johan over.

                    JOHAN
          No rest for the previously wicked.

He winks, marches off.

Quinn's van screeches to a halt. A "Spooked" promotional
image slides open to reveal Chris and Lexi.

Lexi latches on to Chris's arm as they approach with Quinn.

                    CHRIS
          Check us out!

                    QUINN
          Just returned from the body shop.

                    BROOKE
          Are you fine with seeing Chris
          plastered across your van?

                    CHRIS
          He's ecstatic!

                    QUINN
          A small sacrifice -- wasn't my
          dime.

Father Nick circles the grounds in a hard hat, sprinkling a
little bottle while he murmurs.

                    CHRIS
                (calls out)
          How's it hanging, Father?

Father Nick waves.

                    CHRIS
          I know he's been here before.

                    BROOKE
          A few times.

Frank hand signals the count.

96.

                    FRANK
          Six.

                    BROOKE
          Doesn't hurt to ask for extra
          blessings.

Father Nick bangs into a low-hanging beam and hollers.

                    CHRIS
          Better tell Father Nick.

Frank's belt holster rings. He flips open his cell phone.

                    FRANK
          Hello? Yes, this is Spooked, are
          you? Uh-huh. Say that again? Not a
          problem. Okay, next Saturday.

Taps it shut.

                    FRANK
          Who's up for our first out-of-state
          case?

                    BROOKE
          Awe-some! Count me in.

                    FRANK
          It's a distance. All the way to
          Iowa.

                    CHRIS
          Road trip! Hey, let's bring Lexi!

                    LEXI
          Sounds like fun.

They kiss with uncomfortable affection.

                    QUINN
          Where's the haunting located?

                    FRANK
          A town called Villisca. Something
          about an axe mur--

Everybody immediately flees to their nearest vehicle -- Chris
practically dragging Lexi -- and speed away.

                    FRANK
          Real mature. Such unflappable ghost
          hunters...

His voice trails as a FOGGY APPARITION drifts down the
sidewalk with a silhouetted top hat and walking stick.

The Foggy Apparition passes by until Mr. Stantz's twisted
head faces a speechless Frank.

                    MR. STANTZ
          Wrong cemetery.

His vacuous voice ends in a hollow, chilling laugh.

Frank chases after the van, waving his arms.

                    FRANK
          Guys! Wait! I need my camera!

Mr. Stantz continues on. Laughing into camera as we:

                                        FADE TO WHITE.

          THE END

ABOUT THE SCREENWRITER

Michael E. Berg is an acclaimed screenwriter and award-winning independent producer who graduated from the University of Northern Iowa. He divides his free time between watching film and crafting stories, though has a tendency towards procrastination as much as being a methodical perfectionist. Michael resides in central Iowa with his wife and three children.

Find him on the vast digital landscape @writtenbyberg or spilledinkcinema.com.

120pages